MURDER ON THE ATLANTIC

PENELOPE BANKS MURDER MYSTERIES
BOOK 11

COLETTE CLARK

DESCRIPTION

A murder on the high seas!

Atlantic Ocean 1926
Having sent Jane and Alfred off on their honeymoon, Penelope "Pen" Banks and her other friends are soon off on their own voyage across the Atlantic for a few months in Europe.

Unfortunately, the rumor of a maid's disappearance during the maiden voyage of their ship has their bon voyage feeling rather tainted. While the crew is in denial about what happened, the drama among her fellow passengers is enough to create a distraction.

This includes a ghost from Penelope's reckless youth spent in Spain: Raul García. He is intent on making his own waves between Richard and Penelope, by attempting to pick up where they once left off. At least until a passenger is murdered...and Raul is the only plausible suspect.

Soon, the ship's past also clashes with its present when it

turns out both murders may be related. Raul makes Penelope an offer she can't refuse, if only she'll clear his name and find out who is really guilty of both crimes.

Murder on the Atlantic is the eleventh book in the Penelope Banks Murder Mysteries series set in the 1920s. Join her and her friends as they set sail from New York to Europe.

CHAPTER ONE

"THE WEDDING WAS ABSOLUTELY PERFECT."

The newly minted Jane Paisley (née Pugley), hugged Penelope "Pen" Banks so tightly she feared there might be an accidental murder. Probably not the most auspicious start to her life with her new husband, Alfred Paisley. It wasn't such an idle thought considering the newlywed couple had met over another murder the year prior.

"We have you to thank for everything," Jane said, releasing Penelope.

"Applesauce. Obviously the wedding wouldn't have happened without you two taking your vows," Pen said, giving Alfred a wink. As maid of honor, she had been pleased to see Alfie's adoration for the bride reflected in his lovely green eyes from behind his spectacles. "I simply provided a few of the trimmings, you two lovebirds did all the work."

Jane, Penelope's associate at her private investigative business, and Alfred Paisley were finally married and would be off on a ship to France, eventually ending in Paris for their honeymoon. That was, of course, after a night's stay at The Plaza Hotel.

Yes, Penelope had paid for everything from Jane's wedding dress, a white French lace overdress atop a white silk dress with a Juliet cap veil made of long tulle, held in place by a crown of freshwater pearl flowers to the copious amounts of champagne at the reception. The banquet room of the restaurant—which had been paid extra to ignore the contraband liquor—was festooned with flowers and satin ribbons and a *mostly* cheerful air.

It wasn't as though Jane's parents were going to contribute anything. After offering another congratulations, Penelope moved on to allow the other guests to offer theirs. Her eyes inadvertently fell on the Pugleys, who had stayed seated rather than offer well wishes to their daughter. Jane rarely spoke about her parents, and Penelope could finally see why. The frowns presently on their faces were identical to the ones they'd sported throughout the ceremony. Perhaps it was the fact that their daughter hadn't gone running back home to Poughkeepsie as they'd assumed she would. Or perhaps because it was Jane's second marriage, not that they had approved of the first.

"I suppose I should take credit for those sour looks. I doubt Jane's folks knew they'd be attending a wedding with an *integrated* guest list," Lucille "Lulu" Simmons said, sidling up to Penelope with a smirk. She lifted her glass towards them. That had their lips puckering with even more tart disapproval. Lulu was a jazz singer at the Peacock Club, or once had been. Only recently, both she and Pen had become *personae non gratae* at their favorite haunt after the manner in which Pen's last case had ended.

"Don't worry, Lulu, it isn't you. I suspect those two would turn their noses up at meeting President Coolidge himself." Feeling delightfully mischievous, Pen laughed and lifted her own glass toward Jane's parents in solidarity with both Lulu and Jane.

Alfie's family, on the other hand, seemed to adore the newest addition to their family, heartily approving of Jane. His parents, younger sister, and older brother were polite and pleasant enough, though somewhat reserved. Still, their noses remained perfectly level while observing the other guests at the reception. They had even raised a glass of champagne in a toast to the married couple.

"My, my, Jane's parents seem fit to positively die," Benny Davenport said, joining them. "Who could be that dour when there's so much champagne to be had? This is a wedding, not a wake, doves."

"It is rather surprising no one has been murdered yet."

The three of them turned to give Katherine "Kitty" Andrews looks that ranged from aghast to censuring. Perhaps Pen shouldn't have ordered quite so much champagne for the wedding. Kitty was already far too ossified for proper etiquette. Blessedly, they had all moved far enough out of the way so the happy couple hadn't heard her.

"Kitty! Murder is hardly the proper topic of discussion for a wedding reception," Penelope admonished. Never mind that she'd just had a similar fleeting thought herself. Some things should be kept firmly to oneself.

Unfortunately, that was the exact moment Pen's older Cousin Cordelia joined them.

"Murder?" Cousin Cordelia fanned herself as though becoming faint. She took another long sip of her champagne —an adequate substitute for her "medicinal" brandy—to settle her rattled nerves.

"My apologies," Kitty said, a champagne-tinged slur to

her voice. "Though...you do have to admit, I have inadvertently helped you solve quite a few murder cases."

"Inadvertently?" Pen repeated with a cynical glance. As a reporter, first for the *New York Tattle*, and now the *New York Register*, Kitty had a way of weaseling her way into Pen's cases. Jane had, of course, invited her to the wedding, as she rarely took issue with anyone.

Considering the joyous occasion, Penelope decided not to respond to Kitty in the manner that she deserved. She had been rather irked to find out that Kitty had managed to get her own First Class ticket aboard the *Lumière-de-France*, the same ship Pen and her friends would be taking to spend the summer in Europe. Kitty *claimed* it was for the newspaper, a story about what it was like to travel aboard the newest and most modern ship in the French line.

"Perhaps I should rethink spending ten days on the Atlantic with you. It seems together we make a rather dangerous combination," Penelope said before sighing with exaggerated regret. "And I was so looking forward to Europe."

"Don't you dare leave me on a ship in the middle of the ocean with this one," Benny protested. His feud with Kitty was mostly in jest after so long, though Pen did still often have to play peacemaker.

"Now, now, you two," Pen scolded. "Please try not to kill each other before we've even departed."

"No more talk of murder. Jane and Alfred are about to cut the cake," Cousin Cordelia said.

"What's this about murder?" Richard Prescott, a detective with the NYPD—currently on administrative leave—finally joined them after chatting with some of Alfred's friends.

"Oh no you don't. You've officially removed your detective's hat," Pen said, nodding toward the glass of champagne in his hand.

"It isn't as though I can be any more suspended than I already am." Despite his lighthearted tone, Pen noted the slight twitch in his jaw as it became taut. She knew he didn't blame her for his administrative leave—frankly, the State Department and one or two crime families in New York deserved most of the blame—but she couldn't help feeling guilty all the same.

"This Prohibition business *has* become quite tedious," Benny lamented. "I can't wait to have a proper drink in a bar or café out in the open without shame."

"When have you ever felt shame?" Kitty quipped with a sharp laugh.

"Certainly more than some," he retorted, sharply arching an eyebrow her way.

"I think I adore this rebellious side of you," Pen said, ignoring them and wrapping her arms around Richard. She tilted her head up towards him, and he took advantage of the moment to kiss her. That eroded most of her concerns.

Perhaps it was the wedding, or maybe just the champagne, but she was feeling rather amorous. Penelope had a sense the next few months in Europe might have quite the impact on their relationship, all for the better. They might even decide it was time to finally get married themselves, something they'd both had reason to hold off on for the time being.

Penelope broke the kiss to pull away and admire his handsome face. Richard had strong features, but the hard lines of his face were softened with rich dark eyes framed by thick lashes. The only flaw, which Pen by now considered a striking asset, was the burn scar rising up from his collar to the right side of his jaw and ending just below his ear, a souvenir of the Great War.

"Behave, you two, the bride and groom are about to start," Cousin Cordelia chided.

Everyone composed themselves to watch the happy couple complete yet another wedding rite and cut the first slice from the cake, an impressive three-tiered delight. Penelope felt rather pleased with how everything had turned out. She and her friends would eventually meet up with Jane and Alfie in Paris after lingering in the Côte d'Azur for a while.

"She'll finally get to see Paris," Pen murmured. She knew it had been a dream of Jane's.

"Nothing like *gay Paree* to ignite that lover's spark," Benny said with a devilish smirk, never one to miss an opportunity for a double entendre, even if very few people those days understood the second meaning implied.

"Here's to the French," Lulu said, laughing softly and lifting her glass of champagne toward him.

"Vive La France!" Kitty said a bit more boisterously, tapping her glass to Lulu's.

"Emphasis on '*vive*,'" Pen said, arching an eyebrow. Considering Kitty was right about them coming together when a murder took place, the French word for "live" was something to aim for. Then again, they could just be jinxing things.

CHAPTER TWO

MEANWHILE ON THE ATLANTIC...

MARIE BLANCHET STARED OUT AT THE DARK, ENDLESS ocean from the bow of the ship. She hated this part of working on an ocean liner, the knowledge that there was no land for hundreds of kilometers. The ocean wind whipped her hair around, strands practically white when lit by the ship and contrasted against the moonless night and ebony water.

Many of her fellow staff members aboard the *Lumière-de-France* disliked the cramped quarters in the belly of the ship. There were no windows and four to a room, and *that* was when one had a chance to sleep. However, Marie felt secure down there, snug in the tiny bed, even underneath Léa who snored something awful. Down there, she could at least see and touch her surroundings.

Up on the open deck, there was nothing but emptiness as far as she could see. She looked over the railings and just barely saw the outline of the huge anchor sticking out from the side. She'd be glad when that anchor was firmly in the water tomorrow. She couldn't wait to see the lights and buildings of New York City.

Marie gave up trying to keep her short, shingled bob in place. The person she was meeting certainly wouldn't care about the state of her hair. Thinking about that, she shuddered and wrapped her arms around herself. A mild feeling of dread crawled up her spine as the wind and ocean roared around her, nearly deafening. She shook it off, assuring herself that everything would be fine.

The only problem she could see was getting caught where she shouldn't have been. The final party had ended over an hour ago, so hopefully most of the passengers and crew were sleeping. Still, Marie wasn't allowed on this deck of the ship, at least not for personal business. That pretentious Gerard Canard (a silly surname that invited the duck jokes the staff made about him) who oversaw the hospitality staff had been quite strict about that. How sad to have your family named after a bird.

"*Coin, coin,*" Marie softly squawked, imitating a duck in her native French way. She thought of Hugo, one of the bartenders who liked to make the girls, and Marie in particular, laugh by doing a very good impression of Monsieur Canard's nasally, self-important voice. She indulged his advances with a smile or flirtatious remark. Marie had learned early on in life that it didn't hurt to have men think you liked them, as they'd be willing to do favors for you...or tell you things they shouldn't.

"*Coin, coin*, Marie, you are not to be on this deck, *coin, coin!*" Marie laughed to herself. She wasn't so bad at imitation herself.

Soon she wouldn't have to worry about Gerard or anyone else on this ship, at least after the return trip home. She had only taken the job as a way to make money and visit New York. Growing up in Calais, she had learned enough English catering to British tourists and then the soldiers who lingered before crossing the English Channel home after the war. That's what had landed her the job aboard the *Lumière-de-France*, where she'd discovered the Americans were far more generous with their money. The tips alone were certainly enough to compensate for the meager pay she was getting. Now, it seemed she'd be making much more than she originally thought, even beyond the American tips. At least if things went according to plan.

"Let's get this over with. What is it you want from me?"

Marie was startled at the sound of that voice, even though she had been expecting it. She spun around, trying to settle her rapidly beating heart. She saw no reason to make small talk or chat.

"Five thousand dollars—*American* dollars," Marie said, making sure there was no stutter or uncertainty in her voice. They could have the money wired while the ship was docked in New York.

"Is there any other kind?"

Marie ignored the condescension laced in that retort. With what she had inadvertently discovered she could understand why they would be resentful toward her.

"I don't have that kind of money with me on board. Though, I do have francs, if you would rather...?"

Marie sneered with contempt, not bothering to answer that. Everyone knew how weak the franc was compared to the American dollar. When the ship had left, it had already been twenty francs to one dollar, and could be even worse by the time they arrived. No, she was smart enough to demand the certainty of dollars. That should be enough to move to Paris when she returned. Enough to find a nice place to live and to get settled into a better job. With ten days in New York, she could even do some shopping and visit the infamous speakeasies she'd heard about.

"Fine then, when we get to New York, I will visit a bank and get the money for you."

Could she trust them? "I wouldn't try anything. I've left a letter with someone on board, should anything happen to me."

Anger flashed in the eyes that were already piercing her. "Why would you do that?"

"Protection," Marie said, swallowing hard. "If you don't pay me, or if something happens to me, I've instructed them to open it and your secret will be revealed."

A tilt of the head in consideration, wondering if Marie was telling the truth. "I think you're lying."

"I...I'm not." She tried to sound confident, but she heard the stutter in her own voice.

"One thing I've learned, Marie, is how to deceive. I've also learned how to read people. I can tell when someone is lying. You're good at snooping I see, but you should have learned to better hone your skills of deception. You haven't told a soul about this."

"I've told people on board enough. I have friends on board, and not just with the staff and crew. One of them will figure it out if you do something to me. They'll tell people once they get back to France." She had some hope that would secure her safety.

At least until the person she now realized wasn't going to pay her came closer to her...too close. Suddenly, she knew why they had chosen that location, the upper deck, well away from anything else on board.

"I suppose it's a good thing I'm booked on the return

trip. That should give me time to discover if you're telling the truth. As for you, Marie, well, I'm afraid *you* won't be making it back to France."

The sun slipped past the horizon, replacing a moon that had failed to make an appearance the night before. Eventually, it hit just the right spot to pierce the tiny opening of the curtains that weren't quite closed in the Platinum Suite of the *Lumière-de-France*. Russell Archer's eyes blinked open when a single ray assaulted his eyelids. He groaned something unintelligible.

The ship's final party the night before had been a humdinger of a bash. The last overindulgence of legal champagne and other booze before they reached the shores of New York. Once there, he'd have to resign himself to drinking at the Excelsior Club or some speakeasy. He wondered if his old haunts were still open after a year spent in Europe. He'd heard about the one under the tobacco shop on 34th Street closing down after some hoo-ha about a bank robbery. How many of the others had been raided?

He sighed, already missing Europe, a sentiment he'd never admit to anyone. He was a proud American through and through. This, despite that idiotic Prohibition business, one of the country's few failings. That was the problem when you let men in office be swayed by a bunch of overly pious busybodies, mostly women (naturally)!

He sat up. Instantly the carpenters went to work in his head, which only made his mood worsen. He knew the proper cure for that. Hair of the dog would work its magic lickety-split. He might as well indulge while he could. The bar on the ship was never closed, one of the few things the French got right, though he'd been told that was the expat American influence at work. Unfortunately at noon, when they reached New York waters, all alcohol on the ship would be cut off.

Russell groaned again as he slid across the gray, silk sheets, the rest of his body not feeling so swell either. He reached over to turn on the lamp next to his side of the bed. There was a small clock there which told him it was already a quarter past eleven.

"*What the...?*"

His outraged voice was loud enough to stir his wife awake. Evie moaned, no doubt feeling the same construction work in her head, and squinted one eye open.

"What is it, dear?"

"It's well past eleven is what it is! How the heck did we sleep so late? We even missed breakfast!"

"Eleven?" Evie said with sleepy surprise. "That *is* awfully late. Marie should have been here hours ago."

"Who the heck is Marie?"

"The maid for our suite, dear." She yawned. "I specifically asked her to come to the room at eight to help me get ready and properly pack our suitcases. Perhaps she let us sleep in because of last night's party."

"I don't want to sleep in, *dagnabbit*! I want a drink to get rid of this blasted hangover. And now I'm in danger of not getting one because some maid wants to avoid doing her job on her last day. By the time I get dressed, the bar may be closed."

"Relax, dear. We can call for Georges to send a drink or even a full bottle to the room. There's still plenty of time for that. I'll have him send Marie up to help us while he's at it."

"The point *is* I shouldn't have to call for a drink. I

wanted to go down to the bar." He mostly wanted one last look at the dames in those slinky black dresses and long gloves who worked in the bar, but he saw no reason to tell his wife that. "When a maid is supposed to come to the room by eight, she should be here by eight! I fully plan on giving Georges, or whoever a good earful about this *Marie.*"

"Well, that's a fine thing. Get someone fired on their last day?"

"I didn't pay for a First Class suite only to watch someone fall down on the job, Evie. I suppose that's what we get for going French."

She gave him a wry look. "You certainly didn't mind *going French* when we were in Paris. How many *Maries* did you enjoy at those shows of yours?"

"Don't start now, Evie. Not when I'm still recovering from last night. Where's that darn phone so I can call for a drink?" He got up and stumbled his way to where he knew it was, stubbing his toe and hissing out a curse on the way.

Evie sighed and her head fell back onto the pillow. She was in no mood to argue with her husband, as she too had indulged in more champagne than she should have last night. Though, she did have to agree it was rather neglectful of Marie not to come by at the requested time. Now, she'd be scrambling to make sure everything was properly packed all while making herself presentable. They'd been gone for a year and Evie wanted to look her absolute best when she made her official return to New York. Gloria White would no doubt notice the *tiny* bit of weight she'd put on from all those delightful French pastries—desserts were a weakness of hers.

Suddenly, Evie was in a foul mood as well. At the very least, Marie should have known they'd want extra time to prepare themselves. Evie had specifically asked for Marie as she was such a good listener. It truly was hard to find good help. Perhaps it was a good thing for Russell to make an official complaint about her. The ship's maiden voyage had been nearly perfect otherwise. How sad it had to end so regrettably, all because of a missing maid.

CHAPTER THREE

PRESENT DAY

THERE WAS AN AIR OF RESTRAINED EXCITEMENT ON the day of departure. It was a dazzlingly sunny New York morning, the bright blue sky creating the perfect backdrop for the promising adventure ahead. Penelope, Cousin Cordelia, Lulu, and Benny all rode in the same car to Pier 88 where the *Lumière-de-France* was docked. Richard had claimed he needed to arrive separately, as he had affairs to finalize and didn't want to delay them on his account. His vague excuse did nothing to reassure Penelope that everything was entirely copacetic between them. The only possible points of contention she could fathom were either his resentment about being put on administrative leave or the difference in their wealth, something which they had never discussed.

Perhaps it was a good thing Richard was arriving separately. Leonard, Penelope's chauffeur, had insisted they arrive in style, selecting the Rolls Royce Silver Ghost. It was his final duty for her until they returned. Pen wasn't sure what his plans were while they were gone, but she had an idea what a tomcat like Leonard, with devilish blue eyes and a wicked smile, could get up to. Particularly if he had idle time, free use of her very nice cars, and the advance pay to cover the months she'd be gone.

Everyone had wisely sent their luggage ahead of time. Penelope *may* have indulged in a wee shopping spree to make sure she sported the latest fashions of higher hemlines and more structured silhouettes. Naturally, shopping would be on the agenda when she finally reached Paris, but it helped to at least look the part upon arrival. She had no doubt that both Lulu and Benny had succumbed to the same overindulgence with luggage.

"I'd forgotten what a hubbub there is surrounding a voyage overseas," Pen said as the car nudged its way through the throng of other cars and taxis. She was glad they weren't personally burdened by anything more than handbags or valises.

"It's so crowded, how will we ever get through?" Cousin Cordelia fretted.

"Not to worry, Mrs. Davies, these tickets of yours mean I get to drive all of you right up to the ship," Leonard reassured her.

As though the car didn't speak for itself, Leonard flashed their First Class tickets to the guard. He nodded and waived them into the covered area of the pier.

"Well, this is nice," Cousin Cordelia said, beaming as she sat back with a satisfied smile.

"Prepare to be delightfully pampered while on board, dove," Benny said, patting her hand.

In the covered portion, it was slightly less chaotic as only the cars or taxis for First Class passengers were allowed in. Passengers in Second and Third Class had to hire porters or carry their own luggage to the loading area.

Even the usual cluster of press was oddly scarce.

Perhaps all the press had gotten their news about the new ship when it had first docked. Though, Pen hadn't read much about it in her usual perusal of the newspapers. That morning, there was only one photographer with someone who was obviously a representative of French Transatlantique, both presumably there to capture photos for the promotion of the company's newest ship.

A sudden buzz filled the air as two cars ahead of them a door was ceremoniously opened. The flash from the camera had Pen momentarily startled. A svelte, well-dressed figure exited the car, her stance indicating she fully expected the flurry of excitement that ensued from her arrival.

"Who is that? Is she famous?" Cousin Cordelia asked squinting to peer through the windshield.

The woman turned. That gave them a profile view, enough that she became recognizable.

"Vivian Adler," Leonard announced, adding a slow whistle of appreciation.

All four occupants in the back of the car suddenly slid to one side to crane their necks and get a better view of the dark-haired siren of the international stage. Vivian Adler was one of the most famous stage actresses in both New York and Paris, and thus, the world. She was equally as talented singing an opera aria as she was performing a vaudeville comedy.

Penelope had read something about her latest play being postponed in Paris. There had been some problems during production. It had the actress returning to America in protest. All the issues must have been resolved if she was heading right back to France again so soon. It hadn't even been a week.

Vivian wore a white silk dress with a dropped waist and long fringe on the skirt. A lavish lavender scarf circled her neck trailing down to her feet. A matching turban with outlandishly large feathers dyed in the same color sat on her head. She took a moment to bask in the attention of her fellow passengers and crew. She met it all with a smile that didn't hint at any trouble brewing back in France.

A car behind them honked, and Pen realized that Leonard had been too busy staring at Vivian to note that the taxi ahead of them had moved up a space.

"Should I get an autograph for you?" Pen said with a laugh.

"A dinner date would be better," Leonard said, making them all laugh as he urged the car forward to catch up.

A man and a woman exited a taxi ahead of them. The man was young, perhaps in his late twenties with exceptionally blonde hair. It was difficult to gauge the age of the woman with him, as she wore tinted glasses and a tightly fitted cloche hat over her short hair that seemed to be of the same color. A billowing silk scarf circled her neck, covering her lower face. Surprisingly, she wore a long coat with the collar turned up. It wasn't heavy, but the weather didn't even require a light sweater. There was a youngish trot in her step as she hurried past the camera with her fellow passenger, both of them deftly turning their heads to avoid being photographed. It was understandable that most people in First Class preferred their privacy, but the caution of the two seemed a bit much.

"And here we are, ladies....and gent," Leonard announced as he pulled the car up to replace the exiting taxi. He put the car in park and rushed around to open the door for them.

Penelope allowed everyone else to go ahead of her, which gave her a chance to look out at the line of cars behind them, a wrinkle of worry in her brow.

Where was Richard?

"Not to worry, Miss Banks, he'll make it," Leonard quietly assured her as he offered his hand to help her out. He showed far more confidence than she felt, but she flashed an unconcerned smile anyway.

"Oh, I'm not too worried," she said in a breezy voice. She arched an eye his way. "As for you, try not to get into too much trouble while I'm gone. I'd hate to have to cut my trip short to rescue you."

He grinned. "You know me, Miss Banks, trouble never seems to get its cuffs on me. You enjoy yourself over there across the pond."

"I will," she said, flashing another smile. As he returned to the driver's side, she cast one last look out at the cars lined up on the pier, wondering if she did indeed have nothing to worry about. Either Richard would be joining them or he wouldn't. With a sigh, she turned to catch up with her friends.

Everyone with a cabin in First Class on the *Lumière-de-France* had a personal escort to their cabin or suite. A man whose name tag read, "Georges" led Penelope to her suite. She let go of her concerns about Richard by admiring the Art Deco design as he led her down the hallway on the First Class level.

Art Deco was quite the departure from the usual standards of luxury and elegance, particularly aboard passenger ships. Everything on board the *Lumière-de-France* was done in geometric patterns or shapes with sharp lines and contrasting neutral colors. It reminded Penelope of her office, which incorporated the same style, ahead of its time. The carpet in the hallway had a pattern of large gold squares against a black background. The walls were covered in gold textured paper, softly lit by bronze sconces that looked like stacked rectangles. Minimalist, black console tables in front of simple, square mirrors were spaced along the way. Atop each sat a square vase holding white orchids that looked almost yellow in the soft glow of the intimate lighting.

"Here we are at the Platinum Suite," Georges announced in a voice that had a hint of a French accent.

Her door was at the very end of the hallway, just before one turned the corner at the bow of the ship where the very best suites were located. Penelope and her companions had a bank of five rooms along the port side. She had taken the best available suite for herself without complaint. Cousin Cordelia had the Gold Suite next door, and Richard had the Onyx Suite beyond that. Lulu had the Pearl Suite and Benny ended them off in the Bronze Suite. She assumed that Kitty was somewhere on the same floor, but didn't worry about trying to find her. Pen knew she'd eventually find them.

"As you can see, each room aboard the *Lumière-de-France* has been done in modern Art Deco style, every detail taken from the most notable experts at last year's Paris Exposition," Georges said as he dramatically opened the door for her.

Penelope was momentarily in awe of the large suite. It had a nearly panoramic view that spanned the side of the ship to the front. It would be a breathtaking sight once they were at sea. The Platinum Suite was true to its name, done mostly in shades of metallic light gray from the shimmering silver curtains to the plush gray carpet. The same textured wallpaper from the hallways was done in silver in the suite. The furnishings in the seating area, bedroom, and en suite bathroom were all dark grey or black with silver fixtures and accents. The fabric and upholstery was a mix of velvet and silk.

When Georges was done showing her the impressive suite, Penelope accompanied him to the door. She pulled out several American dollars knowing he would probably prefer that to the franc. Her attorney, Mr. Wilcox, who had handled transferring some of her funds to Europe, had told her the most recent exchange rate. It was no wonder so many Americans had gone ex-pat.

"*Merci*, Mademoiselle Banks," he said with obsequious regard, maintaining a degree of polite professionalism as he discreetly accepted the money. "There is to be a bon voyage party in the Soleil Salon upon embarking. Complementary champagne will be served once we reach international waters. You can consult the map provided here next to the door if you'd like directions. Of course, as the concierge serving First Class, I would be happy to personally escort you or provide any other service you might need while on board. The phone in your room has a connection with a direct line to me."

"Thank you, Georges."

He departed, closing the door behind him. Penelope fell back against it with a sigh. She started a bit when she heard a knock, but realized it wasn't her door. It was the door to the suite next to hers at the bow of the ship. She was tempted to open the door and peek out, if only to see who her neighbor would be for the next several days, but she decided against it. No need to present herself in such a vulgar way before they had even left the dock. As it turned out, she needn't have bothered.

Pen heard the door open and a young woman's voice said, "Miss Adler, I have the extra towels you requested."

"Ah yes, thank you, my dear. Come, come, you can put

them in the bathroom," Vivian's cheerfully lyrical voice said. Penelope had once heard that voice sing "L'amour est un Oiseau Rebelle" from *Carmen* to perfection. It was no wonder she was called the nightingale of the stage.

Pen's eyes widened with delight. She was only steps away from the famous actress. She quickly, but quietly opened her own door and stole a look that way: The Empire Suite. Next to it further down was the Liberté Suite which Pen thought rather contradictory. She wondered who would be occupying that suite. Next to that suite, just before one turned the corner, there was a door leading to the stairs.

It felt a bit thrilling to be so close to a celebrity. Knowing that Benny would love this news the most, Penelope exited her suite and quickly walked several doors down the other direction to his suite. She knocked on his door and waited. When there was no answer, she frowned. Surely, he'd been shown to his suite by now? Perhaps Benny had begun wandering or, more likely in his case, snooping.

The First Class level was arranged in a large loop around an internal walled area. That was intersected by a small hallway that offered a set of elevators and a stairway. Pen walked further on toward the rear of the ship, hearing another elevator softly announce its doors opening. When she rounded the corner, she saw a staff elevator and another door leading to a stairway similar to the one at her end of the ship. It must have been another member of the staff arriving on the floor she'd just heard.

If Benny was on the ship, he wasn't on that level. Pen headed back, stepping into the short hall to look down into the stairwell. She heard the door to Vivian's suite open. She waited by the elevators, out of sight, until she heard Vivian thank the woman, presumably a maid, and the door closed again.

"*Well? What was she like?*" Penelope heard another woman's voice say in a fervent whisper. It was in French, but Pen was fluent enough to understand.

"*She was lovely, why wouldn't she be? She even asked me about myself.*"

"*She could be a murderer, Elise!*"

That had Penelope inhaling in surprise. She frowned, wondering if perhaps she had mistranslated.

"*Don't be silly, Léa.*"

"*But she was in First Class on the way to New York.*"

"*She isn't the only returning passenger. Besides, it could have just as easily been one of the crew.*"

"*But all that talk of money? It had to be a passeng—*" Léa instantly shut up when the two of them passed the hallway and saw they didn't have the floor to themselves. Elise turned to frown at her fellow maid—they were both dressed in the same simple black dresses with white aprons and opaque stockings—for being so careless.

"Good afternoon," Penelope greeted in English, a pleasant smile on her face so as not to cause them too much alarm at having been caught. She hoped the English would make them think she hadn't understood a word they said.

They both relaxed with relief.

"My apologies, madame," Elise said, switching to English.

"I was simply looking for a friend of mine. He must have already headed to the Soleil Salon."

"Of course," Elise said. She stuttered out another apology, then quickly pushed her friend on toward the staff elevators.

Pen considered what she had heard. Was someone

23

killed during the maiden voyage? Why would one of them have thought Vivian was a suspect? Did it have something to do with the problems arising from her play? But Elise had mentioned the ship. And what was that business about one of the other passengers possibly being a suspect?

Penelope knew the staff anywhere, whether it was a mansion or a ship, were notorious founts of knowledge about those they serviced. However, this sounded more like malicious gossip. If Vivian had killed someone, or was even suspected of it, surely it would have been bandied about in the press. Pen hadn't heard a peep about anyone being killed. Even an accidental death would have earned an inch or two, as people were awfully superstitious about such things, especially during a maiden voyage. But there had been no mention of anyone dying, either via murder or misfortune. So who had supposedly been murdered?

CHAPTER FOUR

PENELOPE DISCOVERED THAT LULU WAS ALSO suspiciously absent from her suite as well. That confirmed her assumption that Benny had gone exploring and lured her into his web of mischief. Surely they wouldn't have headed to the Soleil Salon early without taking Pen along? With nothing better to do, and still no sign of Richard, Penelope decided to collect Cousin Cordelia—who was, unsurprisingly, exactly where she should have been in her suite—and go to the salon to officially celebrate the start of their departure from New York.

Pen wasn't daft enough to discuss with any of her friends what she had overheard the maids whispering. Even introducing the idea to Cousin Cordelia would just upset her, her mind drawing the worst conclusions. Benny would make it his mission to boldly learn more, dragging Lulu along with him. And Richard would have to actually be on board the darned ship for Pen to talk to him about it! She felt the sides of her mouth turn down with irritation.

"Have we lost everyone else as well?" Cousin Cordelia said, noting Benny and Lulu weren't with them.

"You know Benny. He's probably getting himself into trouble, and embroiling Lulu into it as well. I wouldn't be surprised if he's already found where the alcohol is stored and they've helped themselves."

"Nothing a good wife wouldn't temper. He's such a handsome, charming young man, and always so well-dressed. Perhaps he'll meet a nice French girl to finally settle him."

"I doubt any French girl could settle that one," Pen said with a subtle smile as she patted Cousin Cordelia's hand, allowing her to maintain her naiveté about Benny.

There were already quite a few passengers in the Soleil Salon when they arrived. Neither Benny nor Lulu was among them; nor was Richard, for that matter. Penelope studied the decor of the salon as it began to fill with people. It was done in the same Art Deco style as the rest of the ship. Black, leather, cube-shaped armchairs were situated around square, black tables with brushed gold legs. Lamps with the same stacked bronze rectangular shapes as the sconces were placed next to each little grouping. At night, it would become a cozy, intimate space, but in the light of day, it was quite cheerful and sunny.

The star of the show was the impressive display of crystal coupe glasses forming a pyramid on a large, round table in the center. It hinted at the free-flowing champagne that was soon to come once they distanced themselves from the country that had committed the sin of banning alcohol.

Eyeing her fashionable fellow passengers, Penelope was glad she'd worn a recent purchase for the departure. She had on a cheerfully bright canary yellow and burnt tangerine, sleeveless dress with a loose, translucent vest over the bodice covered in an abstract pattern. The skirt, fashionably hitting just below the knees, was of the same dark orange color with vertical yellow ruffles going from waist to hem. To board the ship, she'd worn a matching hat and scarf to block the sun in a nearly cloudless sky.

Even Cousin Cordelia had finally given up her old-fashioned shirtwaists and long skirts in favor of modern styles. She still refused to show any leg above mid-calf, or cut her hair, but she *had* succumbed to a newer wardrobe. She wore a forest green jersey dress with a skirt of inverted box pleats that just barely reached the top of her ankles.

By the time the ship's horn announced their official departure, the large salon was mostly full. The excited murmur turned into claps and cheers. There was a soft lurch and the ship slowly eased away from the dock. If not for the view of the city gradually drifting away through the impressive floor-to-ceiling windows that wrapped around one entire side of the salon, Penelope would have barely noticed they were moving after that.

"So long, New York," Cousin Cordelia said in a wistful tone as they and everyone around them instinctively drew closer to those windows to watch the city fade away from the stern of the ship. They turned to head down the Hudson River and out to sea.

"It'll still be there when we get back," Pen said with a smile. New York against that bright blue backdrop was an awfully cheery vision to stir such sentimental feelings, tinged with a touch of sadness.

"At last, I've found you."

Pen quickly spun her head around at the sound of Richard's voice behind them.

"You made it!" Penelope exclaimed, sounding more surprised than she intended.

"Oh, Detective Prescott, thank goodness you're here. We seem to have lost everyone else." Cousin Cordelia's use of his title drew curious, slightly worrisome looks from nearby passengers.

"It's Richard while we're away, Cousin," Pen said, drawing closer to him. "He's officially off duty for the next several months."

Neither Richard nor Pen now had eyes for what was beyond the window, and other passengers weren't shy about showing their irritation at the couple taking up space in front of the window. Richard guided Penelope away to a less crowded spot, leaving Cousin Cordelia, whose attention returned to take in her final view of New York.

Richard flashed an apologetic smile to Penelope. "I didn't want you to worry when I wasn't there to join you at the pier. When I was told about the departure party, I figured I would find you here. Unfortunately, it wasn't quite as easy as I'd hoped to get a taxi, and I had some minor last-minute business to handle."

"Don't tell me the 10A precinct finally came to their senses and Captain McFly begged you to come back? Of course, you then stated *quite firmly* that you would never give up the summer months spent with yours truly."

"Would it make me sound less romantic if I said that wasn't the case?"

"It would, but I forgive you all the same for making it on time." She would never admit to him that a tiny part of her worried he might have deliberately missed the departure for the very reasons she had speculated on earlier. "What business was it you had to handle?"

He dismissed it with a wave of the hand. "Forms, bureaucracy, boring nonsense I won't ruin the start of this trip with." Penelope had the distinct feeling he was deftly avoiding the question, especially when he wrapped both arms around her waist to pull her in closer. "I *will* say, the entire summer with you does sound rather appealing."

"Even compared to catching bad guys?" Pen teased, playing along. There would be plenty of time to press him about his delay later. No need to ruin the start of their voyage.

"The criminals of New York have nothing on you, my dear."

"You make me sound so naughty."

"I'm hoping you will be for the summer," he said in a lower more intoxicating voice. "I'm already picturing you in a bathing suit in the Mediterranean."

Pen laughed, pleased to see that much more playful side of him come out. It was enough to erase most of her doubts. "Speaking of naughty, this will be the first time I have a place to myself. No Cousin Cordelia, Chives, or even Lady Di or Little Monster to interrupt us."

He already knew that Penelope had left her tyrannical marmalade cat, Little Monster, and Lady Dinah, his white-haired Persian mother with Richard's parents. As for Chives, her butler, and Arabella, her cook, she had given them the months off with advance pay, just as she had Leonard. Chives had mentioned something about a small cottage with plenty of books in Montauk. Arabella planned to spend the months with her sister, nieces, and nephews in Philadelphia.

"No Little Monster, you say?" Richard said, his brow lifting with hyperbolic astonishment at the prospect. "Now who is going to keep us from getting into trouble by always showing up at the most inopportune time?"

As though on cue, Pen saw Benny and Lulu enter the salon. They spied Pen and Richard and quickly scurried over. Naturally, there were double-takes and lingering stares from those passengers who weren't focused on New York as it gradually faded into the distance. Even Europeans probably weren't used to such an integrated display in First Class accommodations. The fact that Lulu was the only one of her race, even as full as the salon now was, only proved that point. To her credit, she handled it with perfect aplomb.

"And where have you two been?" Penelope chided.

Benny answered. "At first, simply, assessing the lay of the land before the tourists ruined the ambiance. But then I found the most dashing young member of the staff and I had no choice but to prod him for the hubbub on the ship. You know how staff are, if there's a rumor to be spread, they are the perfect butter knife. And my, what a sweet and creamy dollop he had for us." There was a dramatic pause to purse his lips, but Pen could see the gleam in his eyes. "We heard the most terrifying rumor about a maid who completely vanished on the last night of the maiden voyage."

"*What?*" Pen exclaimed.

"It's true," he insisted, his eyes even more aglitter at having captured her attention. "Lulu and I were in the Clair de Lune Bar—it *is* over eight meters long. I suppose that makes it the longest of any ship, as they claim, and yes it's impressive and all, but in New York you can easily find—"

"Benny, are you going to spill or just bump those gums?" Lulu protested, elbowing him in the side.

"Ah yes, well, the dear boy and the other bartenders were already setting up behind the bar—too adorable in their crisp white shirts and black tuxedo vests. They probably know that it will be the first stop for most passengers once this little shindig is over. I don't discount myself from that group."

"I'm sure," Pen said, giving him a cynical look.

"Well, you know bartenders are the *very* best sources for any fat to chew on. Who knew we would be served the marrow of the bone right on a silver platter?"

"Her name is Marie Blanchet, and by the morning of the last day, she was gone," Lulu interjected, no doubt just as exasperated as everyone else at Benny's non sequitur narrative. "They did a search of the ship and she had completely vanished."

"Vanished?" Pen repeated.

"Like a rabbit in a hat," Benny said, dramatically twirling his hands. "Naturally, there's only one conclusion to be had."

Before anyone could state it aloud—that poor Marie had fallen overboard—they were interrupted by a new arrival. They'd been so rapt with attention at the news, they hadn't noticed her approach.

"Here we all are once again," Kitty announced. There was a tiny hint of relief in her voice, but Pen noted the tinge of exuberance in her gaze that meant only one thing. "You'll never guess what I've learned about, something awful that happened during the maiden voyage of this ship."

"You're too late, Kitty," Benny said, his mouth set with a smile of smug pleasure. "I've already told everyone about poor missing Marie."

"The maid who was murdered?" Kitty asked, pouting with disappointment at having her moment usurped.

"*Murdered?*" Richard and Pen exclaimed at the same time.

It was enough to reignite the light in Kitty's eyes. "Yes, murdered! I heard it from some of the staff I've already started interviewing for my report. I wanted a thorough look at life on the ship from all points of view—a sort of egalitarian profile. Very French, I think," she said loftily. "They told me Marie Blanchet, one of the maids on board, went missing the final night of the maiden voyage." The cadence of her voice shifted into something reserved for ghost stories told around a campfire. "She was last seen leaving the staff quarters that final night and she never returned."

"But why murder? Surely, an accident is more likely the case," Penelope offered. She thought about what she'd overheard the maids saying, which hinted at foul play, and reassessed her statement.

"There were rumors about her stumbling upon some windfall. No one was clear about what it was. Some say she stole something, others say she was blackmailing a passenger, and then of course there was the likely case she had found some wealthy benefactor who she crossed somehow. Either way, love, greed, jealousy—three very good motives for murder."

"Why haven't we heard anything about this in the newspapers?" Pen asked, skepticism filling her voice. She turned to Richard. Perhaps that was why he had been so delayed. "Surely they would have consulted with the NYPD. Have you heard about it?"

Richard shook his head. "No, I haven't. But it wouldn't have been our jurisdiction, at any rate. It's a French company, and if something happened to her that night, it presumably happened on international waters. That leaves it in the hands of the French, so they'd have no obligation to bring the New York police into any investigation."

Pen turned back to Kitty. "Why wasn't there any mention of it before now? I would have thought you as a reporter would have heard something about it."

Benny answered instead. "According to the staff, they

were absolutely forbidden from disembarking the entire time they were in New York. Closed up ship, so to speak."

"Probably to prevent it from getting into any of the newspapers. But surely some of the passengers would have reported about it?" Pen said.

"I imagine those in charge would have kept that information from the passengers, and for good reason. No need to have a panic on board," Richard said. "If she only went missing the final night, that was probably not enough time for any of them to miss her. Any passenger who may have asked after her was probably told she was ill or otherwise indisposed."

"She's somewhere in the Atlantic now. We may be passing over her final resting place as we speak," Kitty said in an eerie voice.

"Don't be morbid, Kitty," Penelope scolded. Her mind was reeling with this information, especially when combined with what she had heard from the two maids.

It was something to ponder, perhaps even investigate?

Penelope shook her head, dismissing the idea. The authorities were no doubt handling it, and would eventually discover what had happened to the poor woman, probably nothing more than an unfortunate misadventure. Besides, if it had been a passenger, why would they return to the scene of the crime?

Pen drew her attention back to her friends. "None of you is to mention this to Cousin Cordelia. I don't want her fretting about a possible murderer on board. We are here to enjoy ourselves."

They all nodded in sage agreement, knowing full well what Penelope's cousin was like. She gave a satisfied nod and went to retrieve her.

"Oh there you are," Cousin Cordelia said, as Pen

brought her back. "What a relief. I was beginning to worry you all had changed your mind about coming, and disembarked at the last moment."

"Now, now, how dull would New York be, left on my lonesome without you, dove?" Benny teased, taking both of Cousin Cordelia's hands and pouting.

"Oh, don't be silly," Cousin Cordelia said with a blush.

It didn't take long for the ship to reach the three-mile mark of international waters. A gentleman in a tuxedo entered, followed closely by a younger man carrying a small gong. The older man had a thin, pale pencil mustache that matched the prematurely white hair on his head. Really, he couldn't have been older than fifty, but the silver fox facade gave him a certain sophistication. Perhaps it was the air of self-importance that had his nose and chin a bit higher than it should be. He turned to give the younger man a nod. He struck the small gong in his hands, which was loud enough to quiet the room and draw everyone's attention.

"Ladies and gentlemen, *mesdames et messieurs*! Allow me to introduce myself. I am Monsieur Gerard Canard, Director of Hospitality, here to see to all your needs and desires while on board. We have officially reached international waters. As such, allow the champagne to flow!" He repeated the same message in French and ended it all with a lofty, "Bon voyage!"

A louder cheer erupted this time. A seemingly endless string of tuxedo-clad waiters entered, each wearing a top hat and carrying a bottle of champagne with pristine white gloves. They must have pulled every young man on staff into service for the presentation. They formed a line in the front of the salon, then each popped their corks simultaneously. The loud bang that echoed through the air caused a collective start among the passengers, followed by nervous titters. With that many corks going off at once it *had* seemed disturbingly like several guns blasting. Pen had taken lessons at an indoor range and knew how powerful a gunshot sounded in an enclosed space, even with ear protectors. Presumably, all guns were left back in America, including her own small jade-handled affair.

The moment of uneasiness was quickly snuffed out by the anticipation of watching one waiter walk forward to stand on a small ladder near the pyramid of glasses. He lifted his bottle and poured it into the top coupe, allowing it to overflow and create a cascade of champagne. The cheers and laughter grew louder, even though it was purely for show.

Attractive waitresses in sleek black dresses and long, black satin gloves entered carrying trays of champagne glasses for the waiters to fill. That infused the room with a celebratory air as people snagged their first legal sips of golden bubbly. Penelope and her friends happily accepted their glasses from the tray of a passing waitress.

"Since we're finally allowed to enjoy this without running afoul of the law, how about a toast?" Pen suggested.

"To Europe," Benny announced, lifting his glass.

"I'll drink to that," Pen said.

"So will I," Lulu said with a laugh. "Even though I've never been."

"Well here's to new adventures then," Richard offered.

"And old memories," Cousin Cordelia said in a senti-mental tone.

Everyone in the group tapped their glasses together with a smile, then turned to look at their final glimpse of New York. It was almost enough to put Marie Blanchet firmly out of Penelope's mind. Almost.

CHAPTER FIVE

Dinner in the First Class dining room was a formal affair on board the *Lumière-de-France*. Penelope had changed three times before she finally settled on a pink silk and velvet sleeveless number with silver beaded features creating sharp peaks up and down the bodice for the first night's dinner.

Kitty would be joining their table for dinner. It seemed heartless to have her dining alone all ten days at sea. Pen had made her promise that she would avoid all discussion about Marie Blanchet in front of Cousin Cordelia. The six of them were escorted to a table near the center of the dining room. The place settings included a menu beautifully printed with an Art Deco border on thick card stock paper. It presented several courses with a choice of either Grilled Mutton Chops or Filets de Soles aux Champignons (sole with mushrooms).

While they perused the menu, Penelope could feel the barely bridled buzz around the table. Despite having spent most of the day on other activities—Pen had spent most of it in the bar teaching Lulu basic French over drinks—it was obvious that almost everyone was eager to talk about the very thing Pen had made taboo.

"Penelope tells me you and your husband spent time in Paris for your honeymoon, Mrs. Davies. Why don't you tell us all about that?" Lulu said. Richard was sitting directly across from Pen and Lulu was to his right. She shot Pen a conspiratorial wink. Benny, on Richard's other side smirked and rolled his eyes.

Pen returned a grateful smile to Lulu, then turned to Cousin Cordelia on her right. "Yes, Cousin, it was during the Paris Exposition, wasn't it?

"Oh yes, the one in eighteen-eighty-nine, so long ago. I'm sure the city has very much changed since then."

"But you saw the first glimpse of the Eiffel Tower. That must have been fascinating," Richard said, playing along. Penelope smiled in appreciation.

Before she could begin, a tuxedoed waiter cut short the narration to take their wine and food orders. Penelope ordered the sole with a glass of Chardonnay.

When he left with all their orders, Cousin Cordelia regaled them with the adventures of her honeymoon, which were surprisingly engrossing. Pen had no idea her older cousin had such a flair for story-telling. She could actually picture herself at the fair, tasting the exotic cuisines, getting a first glimpse of technology that was so commonplace in the modern era, such as the elevator and the motion picture.

"As you know, Reginald and Juliette spent their honey-moon at the nineteen-hundred Exposition," Cousin Cordelia said to Pen. Pen knew that much about her parents. Her mother had fallen in love with Paris then. Perhaps that was why Penelope was so eager to return to the city she had also fallen in love with. After all, her mother had once told her in confidence that she was already carrying Penelope at the time of their visit. That was something Reginald Banks would have been appalled at her, or anyone else for that matter, knowing.

"Yes, and I'm sure it's also changed since my last visit as well, but Paris will always be Paris," Penelope said.

"I assume I'm the only one who hasn't been to France?" Lulu asked.

Everyone else eyed one another to make sure. Pen knew Richard had served in France during the Great War and, like many soldiers, had spent time in Paris afterward. Kitty and Benny both came from money, and a European Tour was standard for any young wealthy American.

Penelope was the first to spot Gerard Canard approaching the table with an ingratiating smile. She'd seen him making the rounds to chat with various other First Class passengers. As he arrived, she noted his smile widen as though he wanted to make an even better impression on them. His eyes were trained right on Lulu.

"Bonsoir, bonsoir! I trust you all have been enjoying your voyage thus far?"

He seemed particularly eager to hear from Lulu, so she was the first to offer a wry smile and nod. "Very much, thank you."

"Ah, c'est merveilleux! The *Lumière-de-France* does not discriminate, not like the Americans, you see. The French, we are more accepting. Egalité, no?" He gave a self-effacing laugh. "We have fully embraced the culture of your race. Mademoiselle Josephine Baker, she has been a magnificent success. I think you'll find we French are far more—"

"I'm sure Miss Simmons can't wait to experience it for herself," Penelope interrupted with a gracious smile. His pandering was doing more harm than good for the image of France. Lulu was nearly at the point of laughing, which

Pen suspected would have bruised Gerard's pride enough to have him changing his tune about welcoming her to France.

"Ah, yes," he said with pursed lips, his cheeks reddening slightly.

At that moment a slight hush infused the dining room, followed by excited murmurs. Gerard's eyes suddenly shifted to someone behind Pen and widened with delight. "Excuse-moi."

Penelope turned to see Vivian Adler gliding into the large First Class dining room. She wore a cobalt blue velvet dress with black beaded trim. A dazzling smile was spread across her beautiful face as she basked in the attention, graciously offering nods to those she passed.

Penelope was as shameless as everyone else, following the actress with her eyes as she took a table for four right next to them. It was only when Vivian's sparkling eyes landed on Penelope's table and she flashed a brief smile of acknowledgment, as though she knew they were gawking but she was quite used to it by then, that Pen quickly averted her gaze.

Richard smirked across from her. Benny and Kitty were both still staring, she noted.

"Oh stop, you two, it's rude," Penelope admonished.

"Easy enough for you to say, sitting right there with a perfect view of her," Benny said with a pout as he turned to face Penelope. "Let's trade seats, Pen."

"Don't be vulgar. We have nine more days on this trip, plenty of time for you to rudely ogle her." She turned to Lulu. "Speaking of rude, I hope you won't color all the French with the same brush that silly little man presented."

"I do appreciate the reassurance," Lulu said with a generous dose of amusement in her voice.

40

"Not to worry, dove, the French are going to adore you," Benny said, leaning around Richard.

"Of course they will," Pen said. "You're fashionable, artistic, smart, and by all accounts they think jazz is the bee's knees. You may even find a new career over there and decide to stay. France has become *quite* the Mecca for many an American expat."

"With what my cousin told me about how things were for him after the war, I think I'm going to like it just fine. Hell, if Miss Josephine Baker can make it, why not me?"

"Who is this Josephine Baker everyone keeps mentioning?" Cousin Cordelia inquired. "I've heard people speak of her before."

Benny's eyes lit up. "Oh yes, you'll adore her, dove. She's settled in Paris now, has a new show at the Folies Bergère, something to do with bananas," he said, twisting his lips with wicked delight.

"Bananas? Is it some sort of tropical theme? I do love the Latin dances, so very daring," Cousin Cordelia said.

"Well then, you must accompany us to a show. After all, when in Paris..." Benny said in a devilish tone, looking at Cousin Cordelia right across from him with a grin. The way he and Lulu—notorious coconspirators when it came to scandalous adventures—both smirked at one another had Penelope wondering what this show of Miss Baker's was really like.

"Consider our tickets to the Folies bought," Pen announced all the same. She felt a wild abandon infuse her veins, just as it had the last time she'd escaped overseas after her mother died in the Great Influenza. Penelope had left Barnard College at nineteen, and dived right into a somewhat regrettable few years of reckless indulgence. With the exception of the requisite detour to Paris, she had mostly spent time at various ports around the Mediterranean from Barcelona to Capri.

The waiter came back with their drinks and Lulu lifted hers toward Penelope. "Once again, I have to thank you for getting me out of New York. I think France and I are gonna get along just fine."

Pen thought Lulu might seriously consider staying in France. She briefly wondered what Tommy Callahan, who worked for Mr. Sweeney, one of the most notorious gangsters in New York, might have to say about that. She quickly dismissed it. That cad was part of the reason they were all going off to France in the first place.

"I wonder who's joining her for dinner," Kitty, who had yet to take her eyes off Vivian, pondered.

Benny leaned in with a conspiratorial smile and voice. "I heard a rumor that it isn't just Vivian Adler, but also Simone Boudreaux joining us on this little jaunt across the Atlantic. This business with the French play they are in, *Tromperie*, has caused quite the stir in the tabloid presses. Apparently, it was Simone causing the problems, claiming someone was stalking and sabotaging her, throwing all sorts of accusations at everyone from her fellow actors to the crew, even Vivian. She's supposedly the main reason Vivian went fleeing to America."

"It has to be some kind of publicity stunt, Simone getting a bit too into character just to get people talking," Kitty said. "Why else would they have been on the same ship to New York?"

Pen gave them both a skeptical look. "And deliberately cause a delay in the opening? I doubt that is the reason."

Kitty shrugged.

"Alas, it seems she got a good talking to, enough to have both of them heading right back to France, behaving themselves," Benny lamented. "A shame, I was rather hoping for a bit of entertainment I could write home about."

"Of course you were," Pen said, shaking her head.

Penelope saw his eyes suddenly home in on someone entering the dining room behind her. Another stir of murmurs rippled through the room. Pen assumed someone almost as famous—or infamous?—as Vivian had just entered. She didn't bother turning to look again, as it had been tactless the first time, and after the scolding she had just given Benny about staring.

Soon enough, a young blonde woman came into view. She approached Vivian's table. Simone Boudreaux. It probably wouldn't be long before she became a star in her own right, at least if her acting was as awe-inspiring as her beauty. She could easily break into the film industry on that alone. Unless of course Benny's gossip was true about how difficult she was to work with.

"Oh dear, I don't think they like each other very much," Cousin Cordelia observed.

It was true that Simone didn't offer a hint of a smile as she took the seat opposite Vivian. Vivian's usually pleasant demeanor had a thin coating of steel as she eyed the woman joining her for dinner. The producers must have forced them to play nice with each other for the benefit of the public if they were dining together.

Penelope could understand why there might have been discord between the two actresses. The iconic veteran actress probably felt threatened by the younger upstart, who was probably resentful at being overshadowed by the bigger icon.

From Penelope's vantage point, they were both beautiful in very different ways. Simone had an aloof beauty with blonde hair, pale skin, and eyes that emitted a gaze that could freeze the Sahara Desert, at least when they landed on her dinner companion.

Vivian had more of a peaches and cream complexion, with dark glittering eyes and brunette hair. She hardly needed the makeup she wore. But Pen knew Vivian was on the unfortunate side of thirty, at least by industry standards. The voice that had made her almost as big a star as Sarah Bernhardt had once been was irrelevant in the rapidly growing silent film industry threatening to replace the stage.

A waiter practically tripped over himself to greet the two women and take their drink orders.

"We actually have one more person coming to join—" Vivian began.

"*De l'eau, s'il vous plaît,*" Simone interrupted, ordering a glass of water before Vivian could finish.

Vivian's gracious smile faltered only a bit as she continued. "As I was saying, we have another dinner guest joining us, then I think we'll have a bottle of champagne. Your best label, *s'il vous plaît*. But in the meantime, I shall have water as well."

"*Oui*, of course," the waiter replied. "I will allow you a moment to decide on your meal selection."

When the waiter left, Vivian considered her dinner companion with the kind of smile a parent might reserve for a temperamental child. "You are welcome to join us in having champagne. It's meant to be for everyone at the table."

Simone's eyes remained firmly on her menu as she spoke. "No, thank you. Alcohol has an aging effect."

Vivian laughed merrily in response. "Well, perhaps the Americans are onto something then. Though, I suppose you would know best about the aging effects of alcohol, having grown up in the wine-drinking capital of the world. My understanding is children are introduced to it quite early, no? Some as young as five? I can see why you would want to avoid it at this relatively late stage in life."

Penelope wondered if they were aware that everyone seated at the tables next to them could hear every word spoken. Simone's biting remark and Vivian's equally acidic response weren't lost on anyone within hearing distance, but perhaps that was the point.

"Me-*ow*," Benny muttered under his breath as his brow rose with devilish delight.

Simone wasn't quite as barb-resistant as Vivian. She slapped her menu back onto the table and met Vivian with a level gaze. Her mouth opened, but quickly snapped shut again. She closed her eyes, took a breath, then opened them again, taking a moment to collect herself. A sly smile came to her face before she deigned to speak again.

"I would have thought you were well-versed in French culture, having spent so much time there. My understanding is you were quite the favorite of the soldiers there during the war?"

"Charm works wonders. You should try it sometime, my dear," Vivian said, still in that light-hearted, almost playful voice that showed not an ounce of irritation or resentment.

"I prefer not to have such an *infamous* reputation."

"Really? That is quite the surprise, considering the reputation you seem to be cultivating for yourself. After all, we are here thanks to you," Vivian leaned in, giving Simone a penetrating look. "Allow me to offer a bit of advice, Simone, as I know you have your eyes set on Hollywood. Directors don't like difficult actresses. Tantrums on set are exactly how one earns an *infamous* reputation."

Penelope couldn't help staring now, her eyes focused on the scene at the next table. She wasn't the only one. From what she could see, almost every eye in the First Class dining room with a view was glued to them. It was all Benny could do not to turn around. The look he gave Pen told her he would be pressing her for every detail later on.

"It wasn't my fault!" Simone protested, not at all worried about who could hear her.

Vivian suddenly had a genuine look of concern on her face. "Why is it you think someone was after you, Simone? Perhaps if you told me more, I could help. That's why they insisted we spend time together. I only want to help you. If you would allow it, I could be a very beneficial mentor."

"You would have a knife in my back as soon as I turned it," Simone spat.

Vivian sighed with exasperation. "Believe it or not, I am not your enemy."

"I know you didn't want me cast as Camille."

"True."

Simone blinked rapidly in response, surprised that Vivian would so bluntly admit that.

Vivian shrugged and gave her a frank look. "That shouldn't be a surprise to you. You're hardly the first actress or actor that I've taken issue with. And I won't be the only one who takes issue with you. It's happened to me, and as you progress in this profession you'll feel the same about someone else. In my case, I simply thought you weren't mature and experienced enough for such a serious role. It seems my concerns were valid."

"I wouldn't be surprised if you made it your mission to prove yourself right."

Vivian sighed again. "I'm a professional, Simone. These claims you made about someone terrorizing you, why would I operate in such a manner? I want *Tromperie* to be a success as much as you do."

Simone responded with a tight smile. "They've assured me the problem is resolved. And now you and I are... playing nice with one another, is that how they say it in America?"

"Yes, that is how we say it," Vivian said with an ingratiating smile. "Have some champagne when it comes. I think you'll like our dinner companion. He's a delightful painter I happened to catch sneaking up from Third Class one day during our trip to New York. That must be why he's been delayed in joining us, even though I gave strict instructions that he is my personal dinner guest. He's agreed to return to France and paint my portrait on the way back. We can toast to playing nice, as you said. You'll be in Hollywood sooner than you think."

That didn't have much of a soothing effect on Simone. Her smile remained tight, disappearing as she brought her eyes down to her menu.

"Speak of the devil!" Vivian sang. "I see the third member of our little tête-à-tête has arrived."

"Well, now..." Benny muttered with a curl of the lip as he stared past Penelope to the entrance of the dining room.

Penelope grinned and shook her head at his shamelessness, though she could see Lulu's gaze was rather appreciative as well.

"Raul! Over here, darling!" Vivian called out.

That name had Penelope's smile frozen on her lips. Vivian had said something about a painter. Surely it couldn't be....

No longer caring about decorum, Penelope spun around in her seat. Even if her memory hadn't worked like a camera, capturing every image like a colorized photograph, she'd have remembered the man entering the First Class dining room.

That full head of dark hair, one lock carelessly falling into one eye.

Lips so lush they might have been a woman's.

Dark smoldering eyes that did even more damage to the heart than the popping of a cork.

A face so handsome it was impossible not to swoon.

Raul García.

He didn't own a tuxedo, and his well-worn brown suit stood out among the other passengers in their finely pressed formal dining attire. It somehow made him look even more appealing, particularly to the female gazes following him in. He showed not an ounce of self-consciousness or even humility; that Spanish pride practically singed the air around him.

While everyone else could look on with interest that bordered on indecent, Penelope could only gawk in surprise, and far too much familiarity.

It was only when he sat down in the chair facing Penelope's table that his gaze aligned with hers. Instant recognition touched his eyes, telling her that he remembered her all too well. A knowing grin spread his lips, just before he mouthed her name.

Richard's eyes in her periphery pierced her enough to force her attention away from the man situated almost directly behind him. He'd seen everything...and had deduced just enough to suspect the worst.

"Excuse me, I—I'm feeling suddenly unwell," Pen said, quickly rising from her seat and leaving the dining room. It felt like every eye followed her out, but she only felt the heat of two pairs in particular searing her back as she left. She quickened her step to escape them.

What was Raul García doing on the *Lumière-de-France*?

CHAPTER SIX

"Penelope!"

Despite Richard calling after her, Penelope continued to flee, even though she had long since left the dining room.

"Penelope, stop...*stop!*"

She came to a stop, breathing heavily, mostly from the emotions wracking her body than the effort it had taken to escape. Why had she done that? Of course it would make Richard—and everyone else—suspicious. All she'd had to do was sit there and ignore Raul until dinner ended. She could only imagine what Benny and Kitty in particular might be saying in the wake of the scene she'd just made.

Richard caught up to her, and she spun around to face him. She was surprised to see a look of concern on his face rather than jealousy, suspicion, or anger.

"Are you alright?"

"I...er, yes. I'm fine, just a little..." She exhaled a short laugh. "Just a little seasickness."

"Is it?" He quirked an eyebrow.

"Oh, alright, I overreacted to seeing someone I know —*knew*....a long time ago."

"That man who walked in. Raul?"

"Raul García."

He nodded, his assumption confirmed. Still, she could see the curiosity in his gaze.

"You're wondering just what my relationship with him is," Pen said before he could ask the question.

"Relationship? Is that what it was—or is? Why did you say 'is' instead of 'was?'"

Pen blinked in confusion, then shook her head with frustration. "There is no 'is'—or 'was,' for that matter. He was one of many people I met while in Barcelona. We drank wine and danced and debated and..." She shrugged.

"*And?*"

She thought about everything that had happened years ago in Barcelona. "And nothing," she lied.

Instantly the guilt hit her. Yes, she had danced around the truth a time or two with Richard, especially early on in their relationship. But that had always been in relation to a case, and always for the greater good. In a manner of speaking, perhaps this lie was for the greater good as well.

Richard stared at her for a long moment, as though waiting for her to change her mind and tell him everything, at least that's what her guilty conscience told her.

"If you're asking if we were together, then yes. I did share an apartment with him at some point. I was rather low on funds at the time—my father's way of hinting that I should return home. It was harmless fun, rather bohemian. Certainly you know I wasn't a nun when you met me, and you have a history of your own. I never asked what you did while in France, or in college, or with—"

"You're rambling," he said in a dry tone.

"I plead the fifth?"

"That's not suspicious at all," he said, but there was an ounce of wry humor laced through it.

"It isn't as though I knew he'd be on this ship." She threw up her hands in exasperation.

"It is quite the coincidence."

"Yes, a coincidence, nothing more." Penelope hoped he would leave it at that, even though she now had a moment to evaluate her own suspicions. What had Raul been doing on the original trip to New York in the first place? Was he really returning to France solely at the request of Vivian?

Richard sighed and considered Penelope. "I don't want to fight about this, not on the first night."

"Then let's not," she said, coming closer to wrap her arms around him. "As I stated, we both had histories before we met, let's leave them in the past."

"Is there anything else I might be surprised by in the *future*? Another Spanish beau? French? German? Italian?"

Penelope laughed. "Are you just going to name every country in Europe? The World? We might be here a while."

"That depends. Just how many countries have you visited?" Now he was being entirely humorous and Penelope felt her tension release just a tad.

"Don't worry, Sir Prescott, you won't have to spar for my virtue or my hand. I'm yours."

"Good then," he said firmly, wrapping his arms around her as well.

Pen smiled, then rose on her toes to peck him on the lips. "I overreacted in there. It was just a shock is all. Still, I can't go back. I'm sure everyone already has the most sordid ideas about why I fled."

"They're your friends. Even if they do, I doubt they'll be as harsh as I was about it."

"You weren't harsh, you were just curious. Maybe a bit

jealous." She smiled. "I can't fault you for that. It's rather flattering."

He smiled back. "I'll make excuses for you."

"I'm going to my suite. I think a little platinum indulgence should help me forget about how mortifying this has been. Tell them I'll be at the Clair de Lune Bar for tonight's party. I don't want to be a wet blanket when we've only just begun our trip."

"Are you sure?"

"It's the longest bar on the ocean, Richard. How could I not enjoy it while I can?"

He breathed out a laugh, then nodded. "Alright, I'll tell them. I'll come and get you myself for the party."

They kissed and pulled apart. Pen watched him go and breathed out a sigh of relief. It did nothing to ease the guilt, but that was a burden she'd have to carry, at least until they got to France and Raul was no longer a concern. She slowly walked back to her suite, her mind focused on the nagging little problem that was Raul. Her time in Barcelona was a Mediterranean blur, heavily infused with Spanish wine. Thank goodness Richard wasn't the kind of man to get into a tizzy over her history with other men.

Of course, those men weren't presently on the same boat as Penelope for a good ten days in the middle of the Atlantic Ocean.

Pen reached her suite and came to a sudden stop when she saw the door to Vivian's suite. It occurred to her that if Raul was going to be painting Vivian the entire trip over, there was the risk she would run into him often enough.

"I can manage that," she said to herself. One frank talk when they inevitably ran into one another was all it would take. She'd make it clear that they could be cordial, but firmly distant with one another. There was absolutely nothing to rekindle.

With that, she entered her suite and felt her lingering anxiety fade away. She was excited about tonight's party. Another frank talk with her friends telling them the truth about Raul and her—or at least as much as she had told Richard—and they'd laugh and move on, drinking and dancing the night away.

Pen slipped off her shoes and was about to get undressed to take a bath when she heard a knock on her door. She frowned, wondering if Richard had come back to discuss things further.

"If you've come to—" Penelope stopped mid-sentence as she swung open the door, only to find Raul standing there.

"Penelope," he purred.

That voice. Pen had forgotten how easily Raul's voice, the Spanish accent adding a dangerous venom of seduction, could make one's inhibitions melt. She was momentarily too stunned to speak. He used it as an opportunity to ease his way past the threshold.

"What are you doing?" Penelope protested, instantly backing up.

"I had to see you. I waited until that man was gone to follow you here."

"Well, you can just go away!" Penelope stopped back-walking and came forward to push her hands into his chest. She tried to ignore the firm feel of it under her hands, but the smirk that came to his lips assured her he could sense she was impressed, despite herself.

He took both her hands in his. "After all we had together, this is the welcome I get?"

"The operative word is 'had.'"

"We could have something now," he offered, his lush mouth curling suggestively.

"Get out, or I'll call to have you removed."

"You don't mean that," he said with a pout.

"I do!"

He let go of her hands and gave her a puppy dog look. "Tell me those months we had together meant nothing, and I'll go."

"They meant—" She stopped, realizing she had an opportunity to have that frank talk with him. But first, she wanted answers to a few questions.

"What were you doing in New York?"

He smiled. "I came for you, mi amor."

She twisted her lips and gave him a sardonic look. "Me or my money?"

He casually walked around her suite, eyeing it as he answered. "I won't deny that was part of the allure." He stopped and spun around to give her a smoldering look. "But I also remember those nights drinking wine in my tiny apartment, and on the beaches at night..."

Penelope inhaled and steeled her expression. "Those days are over. For heaven's sake, Raul, we've both grown up. I'd like to think your days of wooing silly American women, as I once was, are over."

He breathed out a laugh. "Wooing silly American women is how I pay my way."

"So find some dim rich heiress to seduce. I'm taken."

"No one could ever fascinate me the way you do, Penelope."

"Not even Vivian?"

"She is using me as much as you once did," he said dismissively. "I will take her money, of course. She wants to feel young again, and I will do that for her, so long as it continues to earn me First Class *comida*," he said with a grin, then frowned with disdain. "The food in Third Class is not worthy of the word food."

"Well," Pen said, walking back to the door and opening it wider as a hint, "you won't get a penny from me, so take your Casanova act somewhere else. You have your answer. I'm spoken for."

He suddenly walked back to her and lifted her left hand, bringing it to his lips to kiss the back of it. Pen's mouth tightened, noting the way his dark eyes deliberately fell to her third finger.

"Mi amor," he crooned before letting go of it. "I look forward to our voyage together."

One foot crossed the threshold and Pen had a moment to exhale before he spun around, his arms already reaching for her. He brought her into him. Before she could even inhale enough to utter her protest, his lips were on hers, kissing her the way he did on those long Spanish nights.

It did absolutely nothing for Penelope except fill her with outrage. Still, she was too stunned at his audacity to react, allowing it to go on longer than it should have. That only encouraged him, and his mouth grew more greedy. She muttered a protest against it, which sounded too much like a moan to her own ears. Her hands came up to grip his shoulders just to shove him away.

"It seems I'm interrupting the happy reunion."

Penelope felt her stomach drop. Raul ended the kiss, pulling away so that they could both see Richard standing there.

CHAPTER SEVEN

"Richard!" Penelope exclaimed, the surprise in her voice making her sound guilty. "It's..."

She stopped, knowing the cliché words she was about to utter would only make her look guiltier. Her hand itched to slap Raul right across the face, but too much time had passed for it not to look contrived.

"It's not what it looks like?" Richard said, crossing his arms over his chest. The anger in his gaze bounced back and forth between the two of them.

"It isn't," Pen insisted.

"I apologize," Raul said, sounding not one bit sorry. "I was caught up in the moment. I am helpless around an irresistible woman, especially one I have an intimate history with."

"A woman who certainly gave no intention that she wanted to be kissed...or renew that history," Penelope snapped. Right then, she didn't care how contrived the slap would look, but she focused on her priorities.

"Again, my apologies," Raul said with a humble bow. "I did not know she was taken. I saw no ring."

Penelope looked at him, eyes wide with indignation. She had made it quite clear in her suite that she was taken. Before she could proclaim as much, he was already leaving. She saw no reason to keep him there just to give him a good piece of her mind.

That left Richard, staring hard at her. His eyes flitted to her open door—from which he had most certainly seen Raul and her exit.

"Nothing happened," she insisted. Another cliché remark. It was the same claim her ex-fiancé Clifford Stokes had made when she had literally caught him in the act with another woman.

"I suppose he forced his way in?"

"He did, as a matter of fact."

He breathed out a caustic laugh and shook his head in disbelief.

"You think I'm lying?"

"Are you?"

Penelope felt her anger set in. "Alright, you caught me. In the ten minutes between leaving you and you coming back, he and I did everything imaginable!"

He studied her, once again waiting for her to tell the truth. Or perhaps that was just her imagination again.

Penelope felt her anger come back. "Since you're so insistent on the truth, how about you be honest with me?"

A flicker of confusion colored his gaze. "What do you mean?"

"You tell me! You've been distant lately. Should *I* be worried?"

His gaze hardened. "Are you deflecting?"

"Are you?"

He closed his eyes and grabbed the back of his neck in frustration. A long slow breath escaped his lips. When he opened them again, they were the same soft brown irises she was used to, for the most part.

"This isn't productive, Penelope." He studied her with a piercing look. "If you say nothing happened, that he forced his way in, and kissed you against your will, I believe you."

She wanted to challenge him—there was still a lingering suspicion she could sense—but she didn't. "And you?"

"I don't know why you think I'm distant. There is nothing going on, certainly not another woman." There was a hint of sarcasm she didn't particularly like, but she left it alone. "I'm simply not used to being so idle, is all. My career suffered a setback, not something I'm proud of."

"Do you blame me?"

"What?" He seemed genuinely surprised. "No, of course not, Penelope. If anything, I blame myself."

Now, it was her turn to study him. "Are you sure that's all that is bothering you? Nothing else is on your mind?"

His smile was too reassuring. "Yes, that's it."

"Well..." she accepted it, hoping he was doing the same with her assurances.

His smile softened, leaving one side of it hitched up. "It seems we've had our first real fight."

She wasn't in the mood to be glib, but she didn't want to fight either. A reluctant smile grew on her face. "It seems we have."

"We have nine days to make up."

"And ten nights," she added.

He laughed, which urged a laugh out of her as well. Then, he brought her in closer. When he leaned in to kiss her, she accepted it. Her lips were still raw from Raul's kiss, and she hated that. Hopefully, it would disappear by the end of the evening.

When Richard pulled away, a thought came to her. "I thought you were going back to the dining room."

A puzzled look flashed on his face before he realized what she was asking. He sighed and tilted his head to consider her. "I confess, I noticed Raul had disappeared. When he didn't return after a moment...I got suspicious."

"Ahh," she said. At least he was being honest about it. She didn't hate him for that. A smile crept to her mouth. "I suppose I should thank you for rescuing me."

"Is that what I did?"

"You did," she said solemnly.

He studied her. This time there was no ambiguity to it. He nodded in acceptance. "Are we still on for the party at the bar tonight?"

"You bet, mister."

He chuckled and pretended to tip his hat. "Until then, mademoiselle."

Penelope watched him walk off, presumably to head back to the dining hall where her friends must have been in a frenzy with curiosity. Her smile gradually faded as he disappeared around a corner.

Raul García.

Richard Prescott.

She was still furious with one, and doubtful about what the other was hiding. Frankly, it was all going to be rather messy. Suddenly the next ten days seemed more dangerous than ever.

CHAPTER EIGHT

PENELOPE HAD BATHED AND CHANGED INTO A DRESS, feathered headband, and dancing shoes, and was ready to rejoin her friends for the party in the Clair de Lune Bar. Frankly, she was surprised that none of them had come to her suite to learn more about why she had so abruptly left dinner. Perhaps Richard had cautioned them against doing that, which made her appreciate him all the more.

Her fight with Richard was still fresh in her memory, but not quite as heated. The past several hours had given her a chance to assess it with a more level head. She could understand why he would be upset and, yes, even suspicious. She probably hadn't used the most opportune time to turn it back on him, questioning why he had been so distant. She resolved to forget about all of it, so long as he did as well.

After all, it wouldn't be *that* hard to avoid Raul, even if he was going to be painting Vivian right next door to her.

One good thing about the party was that it was strictly limited to First Class passengers. Vivian's influence was enough to invite Raul to dinner, but she doubted it would be used just to get him into a party. At least Pen hoped it wouldn't.

There was a knock on the door and she braced herself. She wisely asked who it was before opening it this time.

"It's Richard," he answered.

She opened the door with a grin on her face. "Just you?"

"I told everyone else we'd meet them there. That should give you a bit more time before they bombard you with questions."

She took his arm and allowed him to lead her down the hallway. "So, what did they say when you went back to dinner?"

"You'll be happy to know they were mostly just concerned about how you were feeling."

"Even Kitty?" Pen asked in surprise.

He laughed softly. "Well...she was the first to try and make a connection between you and *Raul*." Pen didn't miss the way Richard uttered his name. "Everyone else came to your defense."

The Clair de Lune Bar at night was a spectacular sight. Like the Soleil Salon, one entire wall had a panoramic view from the stern of the ship, one level higher. Through the windows, Penelope could see the moon reflected off the dark water, rippling in the wake of the ship, and the sky filled with stars above.

The room was as large as the Soleil Salon, but a contrasting vision. Whereas in the salon, the walls and carpet were gold with black furniture, here the walls and carpet were black with gold details and furniture, making it seem more daring and exciting. A jazz band played on a small stage next to a piano that sat idle at the moment. Black and gold balloons covered the floor, occasionally eliciting a loud pop when one of the people drunkenly doing the Charleston stepped on one.

Behind the long bar, brightly lit shelves were filled with every brand of liquor imaginable. Three young, handsome men filled drink orders. Beautiful women, dressed in the same daring black dresses and gloves from earlier wandered the floor taking and filling orders.

"I'll have a gin martini, two olives, and don't be stingy with the gin," Pen shouted above the noise of the bar, offering a wink with the few dollars she gave for a tip. The bartender's name badge read: Hugo. He was handsome enough with a boxer's body and a jaw that was probably a tad too square. There was a jocular tilt to his mouth, as though he was always ready to deliver a good joke or wise-crack remark.

He grinned and winked back as he took the money. *"Oui, oui, mademoiselle."*

"Pen, over here, dove!" Pen dragged her attention away to find her friends sitting around a table further away. The only one missing was Cousin Cordelia. That was no surprise. Her method of imbibing didn't involve bars or clubs, even when legal. She came from an age when women didn't drink in public. Perhaps a few months in Europe would remedy that.

Penelope inhaled, narrowed her eyes and, after accepting her martini, walked right over with her head held high. Richard stayed back to order his own drink. Before she took a seat she made a point of eyeing the three of them: Benny, Lulu, and Kitty.

"Yes, I know the man, Raul who was seated with Vivian. Yes, we have a history. Whatever it is you're thinking happened between us, assume it's true. But it's all in the past and I have no plans on rekindling anything while on board. Questions?"

"I have one," Lulu finally said, raising one finger.

Pen was surprised she of all people would be the one seeking out more dirt. Lulu had always been the one to take Pen as she was, gleaning information on a need-to-know basis. Perhaps because she was so private about her own personal life. Pen knew next to nothing about Lulu's family, her history, and really, any part of her outside of jazz and anything to do with the Peacock Club. Lulu had made it quite clear that was by design.

"What is it you'd like to know?"

"Where did you get that absolutely gorgeous dress?"

There was a moment of silence that was broken by the laughter from all of them.

"Really, Pen, did you think we'd judge you?" Benny asked with a pout, as he patted the chair next to him, encouraging her to take a seat, which she did.

"We all have a past, Pen," Lulu said. She offered a wry smile and winked. "Some of us even have a present. I, for one, don't care what you got up to and with whom. That's your business, honey."

"Though, I have to admire your taste in men," Kitty said. "You do have a type it seems. Once Richard gets rid of that New York detective pallor, say, by spending a few days in the French Riviera sun, he could almost be Raul's twin."

Pen met her with a cool, steady look. Benny and Lulu sported much harsher expressions. Never mind that Kitty had a point, if Pen really thought about it. Both men had dark hair and eyes and at least one lush, feminine attribute that made them even more handsome—Richard's thick eyelashes and Raul's full mouth.

"Don't worry, I would never say such a thing in front of Richard. In fact, consider the matter of Raul closed!"

Pen relaxed and forced a smile to her face as Richard joined them with his drink. She quickly scanned the crowd to make sure Vivian hadn't invited Raul to the bar.

Her eyes landed on the actress, sitting in a closed-off area. It wasn't Raul keeping her company, but Gerard Canard, against her will if her expression was any indication. Vivian's smile threatened to crack from how forced it was on her face. Gerard continued to fawn over her in his fussy and overly attentive way, blathering on about something. Finally, the facade did crack. Vivian's smile disappeared, presumably at something he had just uttered. She met him with a cool look and said something that left him taken aback. Pen stared a bit too long and Vivian turned, catching her gaze. She smiled and lifted the martini in her hand Pen's way. Penelope flashed a quick smile back and quickly returned her attention to her table, embarrassed at having been caught.

"What did I miss from the party so far?" Pen asked in an overly cheerful voice.

"That odious little man, Gerard—oh, he's there with Vivian now," Benny said, looking past Penelope. "He gave his little spiel, then the balloons dropped. One of those things was actually worth being here to witness," he added in a droll voice.

Before Penelope could respond, a waitress came by to speak directly to her. "Miss Adler has requested your presence at her table for the evening."

"Me?" Penelope asked in surprise. She turned to find Vivian looking her way with a hopeful expression. Gerard had apparently gotten over his offense and was once again attempting to engage her in conversation.

"Please tell Miss Adler that I'm here with my friends," Pen said.

"She instructed me to say that your entire table is invited."

"Tell her Penelope agrees!" Kitty exclaimed.

"Yes, Pen, let's go," Benny pleaded.

Pen frowned, but smoothed it out as she looked past the waitress to Vivian again. It occurred to her there might be an ulterior motive beyond the bothersome Director of Hospitality. What had Raul told her when he returned to the dining hall to join her for dinner?

She turned to Richard, who understood her hesitation.

"It's up to you," he said.

"I'm perfectly fine staying here," Lulu said in solidarity, no doubt sensing some underlying trouble.

"The people have spoken," Pen said with a sigh, waving a hand in the direction of Benny and Kitty. She was actually curious to see what Vivian wanted with her.

They were the first to scramble out of their seats before she could change her mind. Lulu stayed seated, studying Pen above her glass.

"Are you sure about this?"

"Yes, let's get it over with." Perhaps Vivian could make it clear to Raul that Penelope was not interested in anything he had to offer.

The three of them rose to follow Benny and Kitty who had already claimed the seats on either side of Vivian. Gerard had presumably taken the hint and departed.

"Miss Adler, thank you for the invitation." Penelope sat directly across from her, with Richard and Lulu serving as a buffer on either side.

"Please, call me Vivian. May I call you Penelope?"

"You may." Penelope wondered how she knew her

name, then realized it had to have come from Raul. "I think I know what this—or rather, *who* this is about, and let me just say—"

"Oh no, no, no, darling. That isn't why I had you join me. It was quite obvious from your reaction at dinner that you were rather unpleasantly surprised by my dinner companion, Raul. Let's not further distress you by discussing him."

Penelope relaxed. Before she could ask why they, of all the passengers, had been so lucky to be asked to join her, two waitresses arrived with two bottles of champagne and a tray of glasses for the table. They popped the first bottle at the same time as a few revelers popped a couple of balloons. Penelope felt her heart skip a beat, a sudden sense of disquiet overcoming her.

"As for why I invited you to join me," Vivian began as the waitresses poured the champagne, "I like to get to know my fellow passengers, at least those who seem interesting. Traveling can be such a lonely adventure."

Vivian's explanation seemed plausible enough. After all, they were quite the interesting group.

"But I see we are one person short? At least from what I remember from dinner."

"My cousin was weary from the long day."

Vivian nodded in sympathy, then quickly brightened her expression as she lifted her glass. "Here's to making friends."

"Hear, hear!" Benny eagerly agreed. Everyone laughed, even Penelope, as they tapped their glasses to each other, then drank.

"Now then," Vivian began, setting her glass down. Before she could continue, a young man came up to the banister separating the raised area from the rest of the bar.

"Miss Adler, you're back!" He had a British accent and a starstruck look on his face. The goofy grin and the slight slur in his words made it quite apparent that he'd had more than a few drinks already. "I'm old enough to have that drink you promised."

Rather than show any hint of being irritated at the interruption, Vivian gave a merry little laugh as she considered him. "Why Edwin, have you finally turned eighteen?"

"I have," he said, baby blue eyes brightening with a sudden bout of hopeful sobriety. Pen almost laughed, and she wasn't the only one. Around the table, her friends were biting back smiles.

Vivian pursed her lips and tilted her head. "You do look somewhat older. And, I dare say, a great deal swarthier than I remember. It seems you had quite a bit of fun during your stay in New York."

"I was in the Hamptons, mostly on a boat." He said it with a frown, as though it wouldn't have been his preferred pastime while in New York.

"I knew it," she said with a teasing pout. "Don't tell me you had your first drink with some pretty girl in a bathing suit who caught your eye. And here I was so looking forward to being your first."

His cheeks—which, along with his sun-bleached hair, did show signs of too many days in the sun—still managed a deep blush. "Oh no, Miss Adler, drinking is illegal in the United States."

That had the entire table releasing their laughter. Pen instantly felt bad for the poor boy, whose red face was now most definitely winning the battle with his golden tan. He frowned, wondering what was so funny about what he'd said.

"Don't be upset, Edwin, of course I'll have a drink

with you. Even if you have shared champagne with another girl." Penelope could see the amusement twinkling in Vivian's eyes. She admired how charming the actress was, instantly able to transform a frown into a silly smile.

"You will?"

"Of course. Though we should both probably limit ourselves tonight. It seems you've already had a few, as have I. After all, I've already had one wee tumble down the stairs going to New York. People might begin to talk if I have another going back to France."

"Oh, I understand completely, Miss Adler. I would never impose on you in that manner."

"I'm teasing, Edwin," she said with a lyrical titter that had him blushing with pleasure again. "And what have I said about you calling me Vivian? I feel so old when a young handsome lad such as yourself is so formal with me."

Edwin looked flabbergasted, ready to profusely apologize again. An older man approached him before he could, not looking at all happy. There were enough similarities to suggest a familial relationship. He had mostly light gray hair, but didn't look quite old enough to be his grandfather. Perhaps Edwin had come along later in life, or was the youngest of several siblings.

"There you are, Edwin. What the devil are you doing in the bar? How much have you had to drink already? More importantly, what have I told you about being more judicious with whom you associate." He cast a particularly judgmental look Vivian's way. She offered a dazzling smile and lifted her glass of champagne toward him.

"I'm eighteen. You can't tell me what to do any longer, father." Edwin shook off his father's grip on his arm.

"You're drunk," he snapped. "We're leaving." Again, he

cast a hard look Vivian's way, this time allowing the steely gaze to round the table and pierce all of her guests.

"I suppose you should listen to your father, Edwin. I wouldn't want you getting in trouble on my account."

"But—" Edwin's father took advantage, hooking his hand into the crook of his son's arm and jerking him away. He practically dragged him out of the bar. Penelope followed them with her eyes, sensing there was more to his father's anger than simply being drunk in public.

"I apologize," Vivian said once they were gone. "I foolishly offered to share the dear boy's first drink. He wasn't quite old enough for the bar on the first trip. I confess, I had made the promise, not realizing we'd be returning on the same ship. But a promise is a promise. Unfortunately, as you can see, his father doesn't approve."

"They were on the maiden voyage?" Pen asked.

"Oh, yes. Though, I'm not quite sure what had them only spending ten days in New York after such a long voyage. If Edwin ever manages to get free of his father's clutches, I shall fulfill my promise to him."

"His father doesn't seem to like you very much." Kitty was the one to tactlessly point this out, but it was exactly what Pen was thinking.

"I fully understand. The Brits are so particular about class, you know. They're part of the peerage. His father is probably afraid of the boy falling in love. But then haven't we all fallen in love with the wrong one at some point?" Vivian gave a small laugh, but it lacked the melodic, carefree feel of her prior versions. There was something sad and distant—and just a tad steely—in her eyes, before she quickly cleared them. By the time they refocused, she had carefully placed the twinkle back in them. "Besides, it isn't just me with whom he takes issue. That man practically has the poor boy on a leash. There was a pretty young girl I saw him try to woo on the way to New York. You might have thought he was trying to speak to Jezebel herself, the way his father cut it short. Embarrassed poor Edwin to a degree from which I don't think he'll ever recover. I have no idea what is so dire that Edwin must be shielded from everyone with whom he dares to hold a conversation, but now that he's eighteen I hope he at least tries to take control of his own freedom. At this point, I want to share a drink with him, just to defy his horrid father."

Having experienced her own version of a tyrannical father, Pen sympathized. But it did bring up an interesting point.

"Are there any others you recognize from the maiden voyage that are on the return trip?" Pen asked. She blatantly ignored the way Richard turned his head to pierce her with his eyes.

Vivian's brow lifted in thought. "Well, other than the staff and crew, there are Simone and myself. Edwin and his father, as you've seen. Raul, of course," She added with a subtle knowing smile. Then we have..." She shifted her attention, looking around the room to see if she recognized anyone. "Well, now..."

All eyes followed the direction in which hers were focused.

"That blond couple near the bar. How very interesting..."

Pen spotted them instantly, mostly because she recognized the young man. He'd been in the taxi ahead of them when they boarded. The woman with him was far less shy now that she was on board the ship. Gone were the dark glasses, scarf, and long coat. Pen could see that she was in fact about the same age as her companion, wearing a fashionable party dress. She looked around the room with undisguised pleasure, seemingly unconcerned with who saw her now.

Unaware they were being observed, he placed a hand on her lower back and leaned over to whisper something in her ear. She smiled as he spoke, then threw her head back to laugh so loudly those nearby turned to stare. She suddenly looked embarrassed, then lightly slapped him on the shoulder to teasingly scold him, which left him grinning with delight. No, they certainly weren't being shy or circumspect at present.

"What's so interesting about them?" Kitty asked, ever the journalist.

"They were both on the maiden voyage. Swedish... Norwegian...some kind of Scandinavian, I believe. Granted, I only spoke with him in passing, enough for an introduction. Gustav something or the other. That's his sister. I was beginning to think that Scandinavian culture had some strict rule about women; she kept to their room the entire voyage over. I only saw her once, and even that was when they first boarded. They also had suites in First Class. Those ten days in New York must have been quite the indulgence. She's put on a wee bit of weight from what I remember. Not that there's anything wrong with it. She's still quite fetching."

Pen turned her attention back to the brother and sister. They were once again laughing with one another, heads leaned toward each other in conspiratorial mirth. Why the quick return to Europe after such a short stay? And if they were Scandinavian, why take a ship that left from the South of France?

The siblings must have felt eyes on them because the sister suddenly swiveled her head to face their table.

Gustav's eyes followed. They both registered looks of surprise then consternation, and quickly took their drinks to the other side of the bar, escaping the scrutiny of everyone at Vivian's table.

"Otherwise..." Vivian, moved on indifferently, looking around the bar. "No one else is recognizable offhand. Why do you ask?"

Pen shrugged in response. "I'm just curious about what the maiden voyage was like."

"Oh stop," Kitty admonished. "We've all heard about the missing maid. She wants to know, as do I, who might be a suspect in her murder."

"The missing maid? Murder?" Vivian asked, eyes wide.

"Marie Blanchet," Benny quickly said, not wanting Kitty to hog the spotlight. "She disappeared on the maiden voyage."

"Well now, that explains it," Vivian said in thought. In response to everyone's quizzical stares, she explained. "Marie was the maid assigned to my suite on the way to New York. I left too abruptly to get a ticket for my own maid. Still, I always make it a point to get to know the help. There is no such thing as insignificant in my book. Marie was replaced by someone else the very last day, which I thought was odd. I assumed she had gotten sick or suffered some accident."

"The consensus seems to be that she fell overboard," Benny said.

"Or was pushed," Kitty added.

"We don't know that," Richard said with exasperation.

"But it is possible."

"Why do you even suspect murder?" Vivian asked.

"Because, despite any lack of evidence, some people seem to want to create a story out of nothing," Penelope scolded, looking at Kitty and Benny. She turned her gaze to Vivian. "Be forewarned, Kitty here is a reporter for the *New York Register*."

"Which is how I know there's more to the story," Kitty said. She turned back to Vivian. "Don't worry, I'm only here to report on the experience of traveling aboard the *Lumière-de-France*. As such, I've been interviewing some of the staff and, naturally, Marie came up almost instantly. They all hinted that she had some clandestine business going on, something very shady yet profitable, if you catch my drift."

"And you think someone pushed her overboard because of this?" Vivian asked, looking horrified.

"It does raise questions," Kitty said. She swiveled to face Penelope. "Which is why I'm surprised Pen here isn't more curious. As a private investigator, I would have thought you'd want to find out if Marie was murdered. And you, Richard, you're a police detective. Surely you haven't fully removed that hat, even if it isn't your jurisdiction."

Vivian turned to face them, her eyes alight with interest. "My goodness, I feel as though I've landed myself in the middle of a sting operation." She looked at Benny, then Lulu. "Shall I assume you are with the FBI, and you with the International Criminal Police Commission?"

"Sadly, I'm just Benny," he lamented.

Lulu took a sip of her champagne and with a placid smile added, "And I'm a *very* distant observer in this little bit of theater."

"And there is no sting operation, investigation, or otherwise," Richard said with a note of finality. "We're all here on a holiday, that is all."

"But surely if there's a hint of murder, you'd be interested in discovering who did it?" Vivian pressed, a note of censure in her tone. She sighed and a grave look came to her face. "When I had my little fall Marie was a lifesaver in helping me for the two days I could barely do anything. I was as helpless as a baby! I couldn't so much as dress myself. I still have pain in my right shoulder when I move it a certain way. I realize you two never had a chance to meet her, so it might not mean as much to you. However, the least I can do is help find out what happened to her."

Pen wasn't particularly pleased with how that colored Richard and herself, as though they weren't interested in pursuing any investigation because they'd never met Marie.

"I'm sure if murder is at all suspected, French Transatlantique is looking into it," Penelope said.

"The same company that allowed all of the passengers to disembark in New York without so much as a word about Marie's murder?" Vivian countered in mild outrage. "If money was involved, it was very likely a passenger with whom Marie became entangled. She was assigned to the First Class cabins, after all."

"Exactly!" Kitty said, thrilled to have an ally.

"I'm so very glad I invited you all to join me tonight. I had no idea, and I fully plan on looking into the matter." Vivian's eyes lit up with a sudden idea. "Perhaps I can surreptitiously question those fellow passengers who were on the maiden voyage? I realize it would be quite the coincidence for the murderer to return, but if there's a chance—"

Richard sighed in resignation, holding up a hand to stop her. "Miss Adler—"

"Vivian, please."

"Vivian, if I'm allowed to fall back into the role of detective for just a moment, I strongly caution against involving yourself in this. At the very least, it could be dangerous."

"Oh not to worry, it will be just a bit of harmless curiosity. As I stated, I like to get to know my fellow passengers.

People have a way of trying to ingratiate themselves when it comes to famous people," she said, as though she suggested a frolicking bit of harmless fun, rather than a murder inquiry.

"All the same, I have to caution you about getting involved."

"Yes, detective," Vivian said with a prim smile that convinced absolutely no one. She cast a quick look to Kitty, and Pen saw a conspiratorial look pass between them that all but announced to the world she would make it her mission to get very involved, danger be damned.

CHAPTER NINE

Penelope and her friends stayed at Clair de Lune Bar until midnight according to New York time, to Richard still had his watch set. Vivian had blessedly moved on to other topics for the remainder of the evening, regaling everyone with amusing stories of her experiences on the stage. Despite Benny's not-so-subtle attempts to pry, she had adroitly avoided any discussion of Simone and her problems or any bad blood that lay between them.

Vivian had still been in a party mood, remaining at the bar when they had all left. Penelope hoped Vivian hadn't decided to follow through on her plans to play the detective. Gustav and his sister had still been in the bar, though mostly keeping to themselves. Penelope had been amused to see that Edwin had managed to escape from his father and secretly return, no doubt to get that drink with Vivian. Pen had a hard time picturing the guileless young man as a murderer, but who knew what was in the hearts of men?

In retrospect, Richard had been right about it potentially being dangerous. Anyone who would push a maid overboard, probably had no inhibitions about doing the same to their fellow passengers, even someone as famous as Vivian.

After bathing and changing into a nightgown, Penelope felt a renewed wind in her sails. Suddenly, she found it impossible to get to sleep. Thus, instead of going to bed, she curled into one of the armchairs by the windows with a book. She found herself staring out at the ocean. The moon hung in the sky out of view, so the lights of the ship seemed to be the only thing highlighting the rippling waves. It was a stark contrast to the vibrant blues and bold yellow sun the view provided during the day.

The darkness that met her now made her think of Marie again. She had gone overboard sometime overnight, apparently. *Had* it been murder? The rumors of a supposed windfall leaned in favor of that being the case. It had to be blackmail. Someone able to afford the First Class accommodations she serviced wouldn't have been too worried about any amount she may have asked for. So why kill her? Perhaps they were worried she wouldn't remain silent.

Still, it would be quite the coincidence for the murderer to return to the ship going back to France. Any rational killer would have remained happily settled in New York, or maybe halfway to Florida by now. Wouldn't he or she want to distance themselves as much as possible from the scene of the crime? Unless they had very good reason for getting right back on—

Penelope jumped when she heard a pop.

She wrinkled her brow and twisted around to face the door of her suite. The sound had come from that direction, but she couldn't quite place either the precise location or what the sound was. As far as she could tell, the walls of the suite were fairly soundproof so she shouldn't have heard anything from Vivian's or Cousin Cordelia's suites. Was someone popping a champagne bottle in the hallway? Had a group of partiers snagged the last of the balloons and accidentally popped them on the way back to their cabin?

Penelope rose to investigate, or at least take a peek. She was halfway to the door when she realized she should probably put on her silk robe, just in case they were lingering in the hallway.

After rushing to retrieve and don her robe, Penelope gingerly opened the door. The only sound she heard as she did was that of another door closing. She opened the door wider to look down the short hallway to the other side of the floor. The door had closed somewhere on that side, but now all was quiet.

Deciding there was nothing to investigate and it wasn't her business anyway, Penelope pulled her head back in. That's when she smelled something odd. She stepped out into the hallway, softly leaving her door ajar. Staring down the short hallway again, she tried to place the smell. She slowly turned in place, sniffing the air. It smelled like something burnt, in fact, it smelled just like—

She saw that Vivian's door was ajar.

Penelope felt alarm bells go off in her head as she slowly walked closer. Just when she was about to reach her fist up and knock, it swiftly swung open. Penelope yelped in surprise, her heart leaping up her throat. The vision she saw caused even more of a violent reaction.

"*Raul?*" Her eyes fell down to his hands, and her eyes widened with surprise. "Is that *blood*?"

In fact, it wasn't just on his hands, but also his shirt and pants. There was even a smear of crimson on his cheek. He stared at her, the realization of what a vision he must present hitting his eyes. They quickly took on a pleading look, as though he desperately wanted to explain.

"I..."

"*Mon Dieu!*"

Penelope hadn't even heard the door behind her open, but she spun around to see Simone standing just outside her suite. She was also staring at Raul in shock. When Pen turned back around, he was already fleeing down the long hallway away from them.

"Raul! Wait!" Penelope ran to stop him, but by the time she rounded the corner, he was halfway down the hall. She watched him disappear down the middle hallway, where he would no doubt take the stairs down or up to another level and she'd never find him.

Cousin Cordelia's door opened. "Gracious Penelope, whatever is all that racket? I couldn't sleep, but I doubt I'm the only one awake now. I—"

She stopped when she saw the looks on the faces of the two women in the hallway.

"What is it, dear?" Cousin Cordelia asked, clutching the front of her robe.

Rather than answer, Penelope turned her attention back to the door to Vivian's cabin, which was still ever-so-slightly open. The vision of Raul covered in red blood was still vividly clear in her mind.

Simone was closer, so she was the one to walk the few steps, softly knock, and call out her name. "Vivian?"

Pen came up behind her, and felt Cousin Cordelia do the same. Simone turned to give them questioning looks when there was no answer.

"*Vivian?*" Penelope called out much louder than Simone had. There was still no answer.

Simone repeated Vivian's name, her voice now soft with trepidation. Before Penelope could stop her, she took hold of the door handle and urged it open a bit more. She suddenly seemed to think better of it, and instead released the door handle and stepped back.

Pen was now even more aware of that strange smell, and could instantly place it. She felt her dread set in when she reached past Simone to push the door open even wider with one finger. That was enough to reveal one side of Vivian's body lying on the floor of her foyer.

Simone screamed.

"Oh...*oh!*" Cousin Cordelia cried, having seen enough of Vivian past Pen and Simone.

Penelope used her fingertips to push the door all the way open, just to confirm the worst. That revealed the bullet hole in the chest area of Vivian's robe. Her eyes were open, but they were no longer sparkling.

"*Mon Dieu,*" Simone whimpered.

"She's been murdered!" Cousin Cordelia screeched loudly enough to wake the fish in the ocean.

Penelope heard the sound of more doors opening, including Richard's. He stepped out into the hallway, wrapping a robe around his pajamas. The look of consternation on his face as he eyed the three women quickly softened into one of shock when his gaze landed past the open door to Vivian's suite.

"You three stay out here in the hall," he ordered, rushing past them. He stepped far enough into her suite to confirm that she was dead, then spun around to specifically look at Penelope. "What happened?"

"It was Raul!" Simone cried before Penelope could answer. She followed with an almost incoherent mix of French and English. "*C'est horrible! Sang!* He was covered in it, *sang...blood!*"

Penelope only just now noticed the red marks Raul had left in his wake. A smeared handprint was on the doorframe and the side of the door where he had thrown it open. His red fingerprints might as well have been a smoking gun in his hand. Like the one her eyes suddenly caught a glimpse of on the floor further in, past Richard. Even from her distance, she could see the same dark red stains on it.

"We're calling the ship's security," Richard said with enough authority in his voice to have the three women nodding in agreement. His gaze penetrated Penelope. "And tell them they need to find Raul García."

CHAPTER TEN

Alfred Duval was the head of the ship's security. He seemed a sensible man who listened carefully to the statements from everyone who had first discovered Vivian's body. His team had searched the room and assured them that the red substance was paint, which was both understandable and reassuring to Penelope. Raul had always favored that color in his paintings. Still, it wouldn't do much to absolve him when combined with everything else, like the fact that he was the only one in the room at the time.

By the time Alfred had arrived, most people on the First Class level were out of their cabins, wondering what the commotion was. Richard had wisely prevented Penelope and Cousin Cordelia from telling Benny and Lulu too much. He'd also been effective in keeping everyone away from the scene of the crime until Alfred, in his authority, had demanded they all return to their rooms.

The Scandinavian siblings, as it turned out, had the suite directly opposite hers. Had it been their door she'd heard closing? Had they too heard the gunshot? When Gustav had opened the door to see what was going on—

much later than everyone else, she noted—she'd seen him whisper to someone out of view. That was presumably his sister, who remained hidden inside the cabin. Pen had also heard him tell Alfred that he hadn't heard or seen anything, and that his sister had been asleep through it all, so there was no need to wake her for questioning.

Edwin and his father had appeared before anyone else from that side of the floor. That meant they must have been in a cabin close enough for their door to possibly be the one she had heard closing. Edwin had been distraught and shocked when he'd learned who had been murdered. Penelope had seen that reaction before, the distress of realizing someone you had only moments ago been enjoying life with, now dead. His father sported a frown of irritation, as though he saw no reason why he should have had their night disrupted by this news. Then again, Pen was beginning to think that frown was permanently etched onto his face.

Alfred was now in Penelope's suite to ask a few more questions, as she was the primary witness. They sat on the large couch, a professional distance from one another as he questioned her. She could see in his eyes that the timeline of events she'd given him did nothing but confirm Raul's guilt. He'd probably already mentally dismissed the door closing as nothing more than a coincidence.

"You called out his name when he exited the room. So you knew Raul García before tonight?" Alfred asked. He had the kind of placid timbre in his voice that could put an unsuspecting person at ease. The slightly melodic lilt of his French accent also helped disarm anyone he questioned. Pen wasn't fooled.

"I...well, yes." Pen knew from past experience the less she said when being interrogated, the better. Thus far, she hadn't done Raul any favors and was rapidly making herself look bad as well.

"You met while on board?" The skeptical look in his eyes was now laced with suspicion.

"No." She paused before continuing. "I met him many years ago on a visit to Barcelona. I certainly never expected to see him again on this trip."

"I understand there was an incident at dinner between the two of you? Both of you leaving at the same time?" It must have been Simone who told him this.

"It wasn't at the same time. I left first, as I was feeling under the weather. He caught up with me a bit later and we talked."

"About...?"

"The coincidence of us both being here."

"*Oui*, it is quite the coincidence. Monsieur García, he was on the maiden voyage to New York as well. Was that to see you, Mademoiselle Banks?"

"No," Pen quickly said. "I mean, I don't know. I had no idea he was coming to America. It's been years since I last saw him, and we certainly haven't kept in touch."

"Do you know what he was doing in Mademoiselle Adler's suite right next door to you?" It wasn't lost on Penelope how he had phrased the question.

"My understanding is that Vivian had commissioned a portrait from him. Hence the paint on his hands. Surely you must have seen some evidence of that in the suite? A canvas and easel? Paint brushes?"

He nodded, with a subtle wry twitch of his lips. "Oui. You said you opened your door because you heard a gunshot."

"I heard a pop," she corrected. "I thought someone was opening champagne in the hallway, or perhaps popping one of the balloons from the party. As I already stated."

Stating it again, Penelope was still confounded about that. She wasn't an expert on guns, but the one she had a glimpse of wasn't a small thing that might not make much noise. The echo in the foyer where she'd seen it would have been deafening. The walls may have been soundproof, but the doors weren't quite as thick. It should have been a loud, echoing bang she'd heard, not a pop.

"Of course," Alfred said in an apologetic tone. "I just want to be certain I have every statement correct."

"What I told you hasn't changed. I have nothing more to add to my statement."

"*Alors*, I—" Before he could finish, there was a knock on the door. His brow furrowed and he got up to answer it. It was one of his uniformed staff and they had a quick, quiet conversation.

Pen felt her heart beat a bit faster, knowing that they had finally found Raul. Of course they had. How many places could one hide on a ship, even one this size?

Both men turned to glance her way, which had the opposite effect. Suddenly she felt her heartbeat stutter. Why were they looking at her that way?

Alfred nodded, then walked over to her. The other man followed him in.

"Mademoiselle Banks, we have found Raul García. He is being held in our holding area."

"Yes...?" Pen said, waiting to see what more they needed with her.

"He has requested to speak with you, and only you."

CHAPTER ELEVEN

PENELOPE BLINKED IN SURPRISE AND STARED BACK AT Alfred. "Raul wants to speak with *me*? Why?"

The member of his security staff with him shrugged. "He did not say."

"Can you think of *any* reason why he would want to speak with you, Mademoiselle Banks?" Alfred cast a suspicious look her way.

"Of course not! I can't imagine we have anything to discuss." If he wanted to plead his innocence she was entirely the wrong person to speak with.

"You are not obligated to speak with him."

Penelope could see from the expressions on their faces, that they very much wanted her to entertain Raul's request. The mixture of curiosity, suspicion, and confusion was probably eating away at them—just as it was for her.

"I'll speak with him." She rose from the couch. "I assume I'm allowed to change first?"

"Of course," Alfred said with one quick nod. Pen couldn't tell if her agreeing to Raul's request alleviated some of the suspicion against her or not.

She changed into a simple frock, something comfortable and not overly fashionable. She didn't want her clothing inadvertently giving the wrong impression that there was anything more to this than a simple conversation. How that conversation would go was still a mystery to her. Was it simply a matter of Penelope being the only other person on board that Raul knew personally? Perhaps he assumed her wealth might aid him in some way. After his completely inappropriate conduct earlier, she was hardly inclined to do him any favors. Still, she was curious.

Despite security insisting everyone return to their cabins, passengers still lingered in the hallways. It made Pen feel as though she was walking the gauntlet as she followed Alfred and his security officer. Of course, she had nothing to be ashamed of. She was simply assisting with an investigation.

"Raul has asked to speak with me," she said to her friends grouped together near her door as she passed them.

Alfred ushered her ahead before they could start asking questions. Richard looked particularly perturbed. She and the two security staff took the staff elevator down several levels, then wandered a small labyrinth of tight corridors before reaching the nondescript area where the internal security office was located. There was a public-facing office on the higher levels where passengers could directly speak with security staff in an emergency. This area, where suspects were held, placed far less importance on being presentable. It was a small, windowless space with two security staff sitting at a desk. One wall held several batons and handcuffs. There was a wall safe, presumably where the more powerful weaponry was held. Pen hoped that would remain securely closed during the rest of the voyage.

It did beg the question though: how had Raul obtained a gun?

Alfred guided Penelope into the office. One of the men at the desk immediately stood up and walked over to a door that had a sliding window in it. He opened it to peek inside, then closed it. He grabbed a baton from the wall, then unlocked and opened the door.

Alfred also grabbed a baton from the wall and walked inside alone ahead of Penelope to face Raul.

"I have brought Mademoiselle Banks. She has agreed to speak with you. As she is not your legal representative, it will be in the presence of myself and my men as witnesses to anything discussed. Everything you say may be used in our investigation and could be evidence of your culpability. Do you understand?"

"Yes, yes," Penelope heard Raul say in an urgent tone. She couldn't see him from her vantage point, but she hoped he really did understand.

Alfred turned his attention to her and nodded. Pen walked into the holding cell. It was more spacious than the office, which made sense. If this was to be a prisoner's living quarters for over a week, there was no need to torture him with barely enough space to sleep or pace. Raul sat on a long, padded bench that was wide enough to serve as a bed if he wanted to sleep. He still had streaks of dark red paint on his hands and clothes, which was jarring enough, but now he also had grime and dirt from wherever he had been hiding when they found him.

"Penelope—"

"Raul, don't say anything that might incriminate you," she interrupted. The wild, pleading look in his eyes made her worry he wasn't thinking rationally and might inadvertently say something he shouldn't.

He nodded, taking a breath to calm himself before he spoke again. "I didn't kill her."

"Alright," she said hesitantly. "Why did you want to speak with me?"

"You can help me. Find out what really happened."

"I—how?"

"You are a private investigator, Vivian told me. You can help me. Find this person who really shot her. Please —*ayudame, por favor!*"

So Vivian had at least had time to chat with him before she was shot. She wondered what else they had discussed.

"Penelope, you must help me. I didn't do this. It was someone else!"

"Raul, I'm not sure how much I can help you. What you need is an attorney, a good one. When we dock in Antibes, I can help you pay for one but—"

"No, no, *they*—" He jerked his chin Alfred's way and glared. "—won't investigate. They have the poor Spanish painter in a cell so why look for the real killer?"

"I'm sure Monsieur Duval will conduct a thorough investigation." Pen turned to look at him, but found his expression unreadable.

"Your painting, I still have it."

"What?" Penelope swiveled her head back to face Raul.

"I will give it to you if you help me."

She didn't need to ask what painting he was referring to. Penelope's memory had every moment of posing for that painting imprinted in the recesses of her mind. The resulting piece of art was an even more vivid image.

"You have my painting? Surely not here on the ship?" Penelope inwardly cringed at how shrill her voice was. It certainly stirred some interest in Alfred, who looked past her to one of his men with a meaningful look.

"I do, it's in stowage. It is yours if you help me."

Penelope calmed herself and asked in a more neutral tone. "Why in heaven's name did you bring it with you to America?"

As soon as she asked, she was sure she knew the answer. The sheepish look Raul gave her told her as much. But the answer he gave was quite a surprise.

"Someone wanted to buy it. A man named Clifford Stokes."

Penelope's mouth fell open in shock. "Clifford Stokes?"

Raul nodded. "I don't know how he knew about it, but he did. He was offering quite a large sum for it."

"You said you would never sell that painting, that it was the one you would always hold onto. Why would you sell it, and to him of all people!"

"Him? Is he someone you know?"

Either he was a very good actor, or he truly had no idea that Clifford Stokes was the man Penelope had met as soon as she'd returned to America. The man she had fallen in love with and agreed to marry. The man she had caught with Constance Gilmore the day before their wedding was to take place.

"That was why I came to America with the painting. I thought I would give you the opportunity to buy it first. It seemed only fair."

No doubt for nearly twice what Clifford was offering. "Why in the world would he want to buy it?"

"I don't know, but it's yours, Penelope. I will give it to you if you help me. Find out who really did this."

Penelope had assumed he had been traveling to New York to try and sell the painting to her. She'd thought word of the considerable wealth she acquired last year must have finally reached him. This was far worse.

Her gaze narrowed with suspicion. "If you traveled to America to sell it to him, why do you still have it?"

"Vivian, she made an offer that would give me the money I needed. I hadn't wanted to part with the painting, but I need the money. Now..." His head fell into his hands. "Now everything has gone wrong. I have no money and I've been accused of killing her."

Penelope was still reeling from the fact that Clifford wanted that painting of hers. Why?

Raul seemed to find some renewed vigor. His head popped up and he met Penelope with a steady gaze. "If you help me, I will not have to sell the painting to Clifford."

And there it was. If she didn't help him, Clifford would have her painting. If she did, the painting was hers. Raul must have quickly realized from her reaction that the last person on earth she wanted to have possession of that painting was Clifford Stokes.

"I don't know why you think blackmailing me with that painting would encourage me to help you. It's a rather dirty play, Raul."

The crestfallen look on Raul's handsome face almost stirred her sympathy. He dropped his head into his hands and shook it with despair. She could hear muffled words in Spanish before he lifted it again, now with tears in his eyes.

"*Ayudame*, Penelope. I didn't kill her, I swear!"

"And if I can't find any evidence to prove your innocence? If it turns out that I can't prove it wasn't you?"

"You will. Because it wasn't me. I even heard him, the one who shot her!"

"You did?" Penelope exclaimed. Next to her, she saw Alfred perk up at that news. "You heard the person who shot her?"

"Sí, *sí*, yes! He was in the suite with us when—"

"Raul, be careful what you say," Penelope interrupted. She realized she was already inadvertently helping him.

"We already know he was in the room. The paint he is covered in is the same we found in the suite and on the unfinished painting. I'm sure we will find the red finger-prints on the gun are his as well."

"It is no secret. I was there, Penelope saw me leave. Before that, I was painting Vivian. I went to wash before leaving. I heard Vivian's raised voice in the other room, that first room outside of the bedroom. She sounded surprised. I opened the door to the bathroom to call out and ask what was wrong. That's when I heard the man say something just before he shot her."

"What did he say?" Both Pen and Alfred asked the question at the same time.

Raul's face wrinkled with frustration and he shook his head. "I didn't hear it all. Something about a maid."

"A maid?" Alfred demanded, leaning in closer with even more interest. "What about a maid?"

Raul rapidly shook his head again, uncertain. "I don't know."

"Try, Raul. Do you remember *any* other words?" Penelope urged.

Raul seemed to think about it, then sighed. "You won't believe me."

"Just tell us."

Raul considered Penelope, then Alfred, and sighed again. "I heard for certain the word maid, but I think he said kill...or...killing a maid."

Alfred coughed out an incredulous laugh, causing Raul to sag in resignation.

"The murderer said something about killing a maid? Did he say the name, Marie?'" Pen asked, undeterred.

"No names, just 'maid' and 'kill' or 'killing.' He had an accent and I was too far away. Then, I heard the gun, so I ran out. He was gone before I got there. I saw Vivian and the gun and..." His brow furrowed in anger and he cursed in Spanish before adding. "If only I'd thought to go after him instead of picking up the gun, which was stupid I know. My paint is all over Vivian as well. I thought if she wasn't dead then I could help...." He left the rest in his head to simmer over and, no doubt, regret.

"You didn't happen to *see* this supposed third person in the suite, did you?" Alfred asked, his tone indicating exactly how much he believed Raul's claim.

"No," Raul said in a resigned voice.

Alfred may not have believed him, but now Penelope was more inclined to. It would have been easy enough for Raul to make up a description of someone vague enough to have security chasing their tails for someone who didn't exist. But he hadn't. And the little bit he had heard was almost as vague, and did nothing to help point the finger at someone else in particular. She couldn't have been the only one assuming that little snippet he'd heard had to do with Marie. Had Vivian already begun her informal investigation? Perhaps she'd prodded the wrong person. Had she stumbled upon Marie's killer and suffered the same fate as the unfortunate maid?

"It was a *man's* voice you heard?" Pen asked, touching on the part that would help narrow down a suspect.

"I believe so."

"Now you aren't sure?" Alfred asked, not bothering to hide his skepticism.

"It was a man," Raul said, though he didn't sound or even look certain.

By now even Penelope was exasperated. Raul may have

been telling the truth, but he wasn't doing himself any favors.

"With an accent?" Pen asked.

"Yes." Of this, he seemed sure.

"What kind of accent?"

He wrinkled his brow in thought. "It was a strange one, I am not sure."

"So not French or American?" Penelope prodded.

Again, it wasn't lost on her that she was helping his case. She supposed she had mentally already agreed to help him. Anything to keep that painting out of the hands of Clifford —a troubling thought she would address later.

"The accent was not American...but...maybe French?"

"Maybe?" Alfred asked in a sardonic tone.

"Could it have been Norwegian or Swedish?" Pen asked.

The puzzled look on Raul's face told her he wouldn't have known even if it was.

"British?" She asked, thinking of Edwin or his father.

He squinted in thought, then shook his head. "I cannot say for sure, but I don't think so. The voice, it was...strange is all. As though someone was trying to change it to sound different perhaps."

"This uncertainty of yours is very convenient," Alfred said, a note of disdain in his voice.

"Not very," Pen argued. "At least not for Raul. He could easily point the finger at anyone, but he's chosen to be honest instead."

"About a *supposed* third person in the suite, someone he can't even state is male or female?" Alfred clucked his tongue and shook his head. "That is nothing to absolve him of suspicion."

Pen thought of something Raul had said and turned

back to him. "You said you heard him speak *after* you had called out to Vivian?"

"Yes."

She turned back to Alfred. "Why would the killer continue talking knowing he would be overheard by Raul? Maybe this strange accent was to disguise another that would have easily identified him." Like British or Scandinavian.

"*If* there was even a third person at all," Alfred reminded her.

"What about the door I heard closing?"

"It could have been another passenger such as yourself who heard the gunshot and opened their door to investigate, then closed it."

Penelope had assumed the same thing, but she was now considering that piece of the puzzle in a new light. What if it hadn't been another passenger curious about what they had heard? What if it had been the killer escaping, either back to their rooms or to the conveniently located door to the stairs?

"You should at least question the people on that side of the First Class level to make sure."

"Yes, thank you, Mademoiselle Banks," Alfred said in a patronizing tone, as though she was telling him how to do the most basic part of his job.

Penelope spun back around to face Raul. "Is there anything else you can tell me? Anything at all?"

He shook his head, more so in contemplation than denial. "I don't understand. I was only gone for *un minuto*. How could this have happened so fast? If only I had not gone to wash up in her bathroom at that very moment, I would have been there. I could have..."

Penelope sympathized. The timing was indeed unfortunate, though she wasn't sure how well Raul would have done against a man with a gun. In fact, it was fortunate he wasn't in the same room as he might have been a victim himself. The killer had conveniently come at exactly the right time to—

"He was already in the suite!"

Both Alfred and Raul gave Penelope puzzled looks. Penelope focused on Raul.

"Did you and Vivian enter the suite at the same time?"

"Yes, why?"

Now, it all made sense. It wasn't unfortunate timing on Raul's part. The real killer had been lying in wait, using the window of opportunity when Raul had gone to wash up to kill Vivian.

Pen turned to Alfred. "That explains why Raul was in the suite at the time of the murder. The killer was there before Vivian and Raul even entered. He just waited until Raul stepped away to confront Vivian and shoot her."

Sadly, Alfred didn't seem convinced. Penelope felt her frustration set in. She turned to Raul, ignoring the man beside her. Yes, Raul was blackmailing her, and for that she should hate him. But she also believed in justice. There were clues to this murder that hinted someone else could have done the shooting.

"I'll work on this Raul, not to help you, but solely to find Vivian's real killer...even if it turns out to be you."

CHAPTER TWELVE

PENELOPE LEFT A TRULY GRATEFUL, BUT WORRISOMELY hopeful Raul in his cell as Alfred escorted her out. None of the security team seemed moved by Raul's statements or pleas. If anything, they now looked at Penelope with more interest.

"Allow me to use this moment to instruct you not to interfere with our investigation, Mademoiselle Banks," Alfred said, giving her a stern look.

It was a caution Penelope was used to by now, and she knew there was no point in arguing. "Of course."

He narrowed his eyes, scrutinizing her. "This is a very serious matter, a dangerous one. I would hate to see any miscarriage of justice because you—how do you say it? —meddled?"

Another term she was quite used to. "Yes, that is how we say it, and I promise not to meddle."

She could tell he wasn't entirely convinced, but he wasn't about to call her a liar to her face. And Penelope had no plans of making a liar of herself. After all, it wouldn't be interfering or meddling if she was to simply socialize with her fellow passengers and crew, get to know more about them, perhaps find a reason why they might have a grudge against Vivian Adler, or more importantly, Marie Blanchet.

"The maid who disappeared during the maiden voyage, I assume at this point you're certain she was lost at sea?"

Alfred simply stared back, a tiny flicker of irritation coloring his gaze.

"I think as a passenger I have a right to know. Was she pushed over or did she fall? Either way, it poses a possible danger I should be made aware of, don't you think?"

He offered a pat smile. "Our investigation into Marie Blanchet's *disappearance* is still ongoing. But trust that all the crew on board the *Lumière-de-France*, particularly in security, prioritize the safety of our passengers." He gestured toward the door. "Please, allow me to escort you back to your suite, Mademoiselle Banks."

There was no point in arguing, and Penelope could take a hint. She exited the office ahead of him, then allowed him to guide her through the maze of corridors.

"I do wonder how the murderer got a hold of a gun. Surely French Transatlantique doesn't allow passengers to bring them aboard?"

His back stiffened ever so slightly in front of her, but he quickly relaxed it again. "*Naturellement non*, they are strictly forbidden. Yet another crime Monsieur García may have committed."

Penelope had opened the door to that one. She wisely kept her mouth shut until they reached the First Class quarters. There was a guard standing in front of Vivian's door, but he was hardly the only person filling the hallways. The news had spread through the entire floor, and even at that hour of the night (or morning, really), many passengers were lingering, whispering among one another about the murder that had taken place.

Richard, Cousin Cordelia, Lulu, Benny, and Kitty were still grouped together as close to Penelope's suite as the security staff would allow. They all became animated when they saw Penelope arrive, escorted by Alfred.

"Oh, Penelope!" Cousin Cordelia cried. "You're back safely. What did that horrid man want with you?"

"I must caution you again, Mademoiselle Banks. This is an ongoing investigation. Please refrain from interfering or discussing it with other passengers." Alfred made sure to give a pointed look to all of her friends as an additional warning before nodding at the man guarding Vivian's suite and leaving.

"Let's go into my suite," Pen urged, noting how the other passengers were giving them curious looks.

Once inside, everyone sat on the couch and chairs, save for Penelope and Richard. She was too filled with energy, pacing back and forth in thought before speaking. He was too filled with consternation, staring at her with fierce curiosity as to what Raul had wanted to discuss with her.

"Well, what did he have to say?" Richard finally asked, exhaling in frustration.

"He didn't do it."

"Well of course he'd say that."

"No, I mean, I think I know what happened," Pen said, shaking her head as she came to a stop to face him and her friends. "Raul said he was washing up in Vivian's bathroom, then he heard her shout in surprise. He opened the door and called out. That's when he heard another voice, a man with an accent. At least he thinks it's a man."

"He wasn't even sure about *that?*" Richard asked, incredulous.

"He was in the bathroom. Here in my suite, I have to go through the bedroom to get to it. I imagine Vivian's suite is even bigger, so that's even more distanced from the foyer where we found her body. Some women have deep voices, and some men have high-pitched voices. Plus, he said they had an accent, so it was difficult to tell."

"I take it he didn't see this mystery man or woman?"

Penelope didn't miss the sarcasm in his voice. "Think about it, Richard, why would he murder her in such a sloppy manner? Plus, he had plenty of time to do it. He could have killed her at any point during the painting session in a much quieter way, a way that wouldn't draw attention. Hit her over the head. Smother her with a pillow. Hide a knife and use that. Why use a gun?"

"That is something to consider," he conceded.

"Also, he said this person in the room mentioned something about the maid."

"Marie Blanchet?" Kitty asked, her eyes widening with interest.

"I assume so."

"I'm sorry, who is Marie Blanchet?" Cousin Cordelia asked, the only one looking around in confusion.

Penelope and Richard eyed one another, then she sighed and told her cousin everything. By the time she was done, she was surprised to see Cousin Cordelia staring back, not with a look of horror, but one of indignation.

"So everyone else knows, save for me?"

"We didn't want you to worry."

"Yes, I may be averse to the more gruesome details, but I'm not a child, Penelope. If everyone here can handle hearing about a possible murder, so can I. I do hope you'll refrain from handling me with kid gloves in the future."

"I apologize, Cousin," Pen said with the appropriate amount of self-condemnation. "You're right of course. In the future, we'll all be sure to include you."

"What exactly did this mysterious person say about her?" Richard asked, returning to the matter at hand.

"All he really heard was the word 'maid,' maybe something about killing a maid."

That had all of them straightening up with interest.

"Very convenient." Richard sounded just like Alfred.

Pen came to a stop and stared at Richard. "Don't you want to see the real killer arrested?"

"I'm fairly convinced they have the real killer. Raul was in the suite when Vivian was shot, was the only one actually seen leaving right after, and then ran as soon as he was spotted. Why are you so eager to help him? Does this have something to do with whatever happened between you two back in Spain?"

"Of course not." It certainly wasn't the moment to bring up Raul's blackmail, not in front of everyone else. At some point, Pen would have to tell Richard that she had lied about there being anything more to her past with Raul than what she had claimed. "I have no feelings for Raul beyond not wanting an innocent man sent to prison for murder. I think this mysterious person was already in the room when he and Vivian entered together. We just have to find out who it was."

"Well, this certainly makes it easy. A man or a woman who may have an accent of some sort. That's almost everyone on the ship, Penelope," Richard said, throwing up his hands.

Pen turned to the others on the couch. Lulu looked

sympathetic, but unconvinced. Benny didn't bother hiding his skepticism. Kitty seemed to be considering it, but perhaps that was just the hope there might be an interesting story in it. Penelope stopped when she got to Cousin Cordelia and saw her torn expression.

"What is it, Cousin?" Pen urged.

"Well...I don't know if it's anything. It may be nothing, but then again, it may be related. I don't want to get your hopes up, dear."

"Of course," she said patiently. "What is it?"

Cousin Cordelia realized all eyes were pinned to her and she at first seemed to regret speaking up, then a bloom of pleasure colored her cheeks at the attention. She pursed her lips and sat up straighter. "As you know I retired early after dinner; the day simply got to me. Well, after a brief rest, I woke up and decided to take a walk on the promenade while I had it to myself, as everyone else was presumably at the party in the bar. When I returned, I saw a member of the staff at Vivian's door."

"A maid?" Pen asked.

"No, that was the strange thing. It was a man. I only saw him from behind, but he was wearing a tuxedo complete with the top hat."

"How do you know it was a member of the staff and not a passenger?" Richard asked. "Almost every man in the bar, including myself, was wearing a tuxedo, some even with top hats."

"Now that you ask, I can't say for sure. However, this person had several fresh towels in his arms, as though he was delivering them. Again, odd. Wouldn't that be the job of one of the maids? I assumed it was some male member of the staff wearing the same tuxedoes we saw on the men during the event in the Soleil Salon."

Pen frowned in thought. Just how many towels did Vivian go through on a given day? Elise had brought extra towels to the suite earlier. Perhaps it was in preparation for Raul painting in her room, knowing that he might use her towels to clean up?

"Why would they have come while she was at the bar? Surely towels weren't that urgent while she was gone. And why would a waiter bring them instead of a maid?" Penelope pondered aloud.

"Perhaps he was called up in a pinch, as no maid was available to deliver them?" Benny offered.

"Most First Class passengers were in the bar. I doubt the maids were overly extended at the time. They usually clean the rooms in the late morning or early afternoon. They wouldn't all be asleep at the same time, would they?"

"Maybe it wasn't a staff member," Lulu suggested.

"But the towels," Cousin Cordelia said. "Why would a fellow passenger be bringing towels to her room?"

"To hide the gun!" Pen exclaimed.

"The gun wasn't *that* big. It would draw less attention to simply carry it under their jacket," Richard said.

"And have an unsightly bulge? No, better to pretend to be a member of staff helping a maid out by delivering towels a passenger had requested." Pen continued before he could keep punching holes in her theory. "I suspected the murderer was already in the suite when Vivian and Raul entered. It could have been any of our fellow passengers or the crew. Most of them would have access to a tuxedo and top hat. And a passenger could just carry the fresh towels from their own cabin. Who did Vivian interrogate after we left? I saw Edwin and the two Scandinavian siblings still at the bar. Then, there was that Gerard Canard. He was on the maiden voyage and would have been far more likely to interact with Marie than a passenger. Maybe Marie found out something that threatened his job?"

"Surely you aren't claiming someone broke into her suite to lie in wait to murder her?" Richard asked. "Are you that determined to save Raul you'd leap to such an absurd conclusion?"

"It isn't absurd. I heard a door close, Richard. Someone either left by the stairwell or into their own suite on the other side of this floor—where both the siblings and Edwin and his father are staying." She turned to Cousin Cordelia. "Can you describe anything about this man—are you certain it really was a man?"

"Why would a woman wear a tuxedo?" Cousin Cordelia gave Pen a puzzled look. It was a reminder of the limitations of her more old-fashioned cousin's sensibilities. "But as I said, I only saw them from behind, and at a distance. And the lighting in these hallways is so dim, you know. He was neither fat nor too skinny. Not tall, nor too short. Light hair, from what I could see underneath the hat."

That could have been any of them, including the very blonde Simone, now that Pen thought of it.

"Oh, and he was wearing black gloves."

That had everyone staring in bewilderment. All the men who had brought in champagne during the departing ceremony wore white gloves. And any man who owned a tuxedo would have worn the same. Black gloves with a tuxedo was gauche.

"If they wore gloves, they were obviously worried about leaving fingerprints," Pen said.

"Did you see this person actually enter the suite?" Richard asked.

Cousin Cordelia shook her head, giving Pen an apologetic look. "No. In fact, when I called out a cheerful 'good afternoon,' they simply left. Without saying anything in return, I might add," she said, looking perfectly indignant at the snub.

Richard turned to give Pen a look that said, *there you have it.*

"Obviously, they were thwarted by my cousin's arrival. They must have come back when no one was around," she countered. She was more than certain that this was Vivian's killer. "It's at least something we should report to security."

He sighed and nodded. "On that, we can agree."

"Good," Pen said, happy to see he hadn't become completely blinded to reason.

"For now, it's late. I, for one, would appreciate getting at least some sleep. Perhaps in the morning we'll all have clearer heads," Richard said, plainly offering that tidbit for Penelope's benefit.

"I agree, we should all go to bed," Lulu said. Her voice and a look that could make anyone's knees weak were even more effective than Richard when he wore his detective hat. With mild disappointment, everyone else rose and exited the suite, leaving Richard and Penelope alone.

"I have a confession to make," Penelope began with a heavy breath once they had all left.

"Do I want to hear it?" Richard asked, his arms crossed over his chest.

"I lied earlier when I said there was nothing more between Raul and me." She quickly continued, noting the look of alarm on his face. "It's a painting. Specifically, a painting of me. I didn't mention it, because I didn't think it was an issue. Raul had possession of it, claimed he would never sell it. But now, he's promised to give it to me if I help him discover who killed Vivian."

Richard's eyes narrowed, studying her. "What kind of painting was it?"

Penelope felt the judgment radiating from him. She lifted her chin. "There's hardly anything scandalous about it. It's *art*, Richard. Surely you of all people can appreciate that?" His having studied art at Princeton was what had brought them together in the first place.

"Not when the woman I fully intend to marry one day might be in some remake of the *Birth of Venus*...or was it something akin to François Boucher's more unsavory works?"

Penelope ignored the way her heart fluttered at the first part of his statement which was vastly overshadowed by her outrage over the second part. She wasn't an art scholar, but she had certainly seen some of Boucher's 'more unsavory works,' some of which left absolutely nothing to the imagination. "You really think that lowly of me?"

"It's not a judgment, Penelope—"

"Isn't it?"

"I just think I have a right to know."

"Well you can rest assured Raul García is no François Boucher."

"So, were you clothed?"

Penelope paused again before answering, which did nothing but cause a deep furrow in his brow as he guessed the answer.

"I was...tastefully covered."

Richard closed his eyes and inhaled. "Alright, that's..." He opened them again and exhaled. "I can accept that. Just tell me how much of you is on the canvas."

"There was a strategically placed red silk scarf."

He waited. *"That's all?"*

"It was enough...mostly."

"What does 'mostly' mean?"

"It means Boucher has nothing to worry about," she snapped. "Rest assured, even Venus is showing more in her little clamshell than I did."

Richard took a breath, then closed his eyes and opened them again. "At least now I know why you are so eager to think Raul is innocent."

"Actually, I really do think he's innocent. Especially with Cousin Cordelia's new information. This mysterious man with the towels. The door I heard closing, which could have been the real killer escaping. What Raul overheard in the suite. And why use a gun? He's much bigger and stronger than Vivian, he could have easily overpowered her. More importantly, what motive would he have to kill her?"

Richard considered her for a long moment. "Is the painting that important to you?" There were a number of underlying interpretations for that question.

"It is...considering the circumstances." She swallowed hard at his questioning look. "Apparently Clifford Stokes had offered to buy it."

"*What?*" His hands fell to his sides in shock, then curled in anger. "Why would he want it?"

"I don't know. Raul doesn't even seem to know who he is, at least in relation to me. The offer must have come out of the blue."

"And what if it turns out that Raul is guilty?"

"Then I suppose we have nothing to worry about," she threw her hands up.

"There's no need to take it out on me, Penelope," he said in a calm voice. "Though you should have told me about the painting in the first place."

"Yes, I'm sorry about that. It's just that, especially after the way I fled from the dining room, I didn't want to create more drama."

Richard coughed out a laugh. "Well, we definitely have a drama on our hands now. I feel like I earned this, having complained earlier about not being a detective for the next few months."

"Does that mean you'll help me?"

Richard sighed. "You know my usual stance when it comes to murder cases. We should leave it to the authorities to investigate." He held his hand up to stop her protest as he continued. "Further, even if Raul didn't kill Vivian, the real killer, possibly of two women, is currently on this ship. You playing detective will only have you becoming the next victim. That may very well be what got Vivian murdered."

That was the one caution to which Penelope had no argument. "You're right, of course."

He studied her for a moment, then nodded and brought her closer to kiss on the forehead. "Let's at least give Alfred and his team the benefit of the doubt that they are investigating this in an honest manner. If we discover otherwise, then yes, I will help you."

"Alright," Pen said, hugging him back.

They parted and said their goodbyes, Richard offering a proper kiss before he returned to his suite.

Penelope was still too filled with questions and concerns to fall asleep so easily. She continued to pace in her suite, her mind bouncing back and forth between Raul and Clifford. Two men who had treated her rather poorly. Two men she had thought she was rid of for good. It made her appreciate Richard all the same. She really should have trusted him with the truth in the first place.

Speaking of men, her mind wandered to the most

important question: who was the man Cousin Cordelia had seen?

Before she could consider it further, there was a knock on her door. She opened it, assuming Richard wanted to get one last warning in before she did something reckless.

Pen stopped cold, her heart doing the same when she saw who was standing there.

"Gustav, is it?"

CHAPTER THIRTEEN

PENELOPE FELT A STRONG URGE TO QUICKLY SLAM SHUT the door she had just opened to one of her First Class neighbors. Gustav stared back at her, his clear blue eyes piercing as he studied her with intensity.

"You know my name?" There was a flash of something in Gustav's eyes, anger or fear.

Rather than answer she asked, "What do you want?"

A short, sharp exhale escaped his lips and he briefly closed his eyes before opening them again and addressing her. "I apologize, but I must know what you discussed with Mr. Duval, the head of security."

It occurred to Penelope that the guard in front of Vivian's door was gone. Had he been relieved of duty so soon? She knew Vivian's body had been taken to the ship's morgue, and they had conducted a preliminary investigation inside the suite. What if the killer returned, hoping they had overlooked something?

What if the killer was standing at Penelope's door right now, demanding answers from her?

"Please, Miss Banks, I don't mean to alarm you but—"

"How do you know my name?" Penelope asked with quite a bit of alarm.

"I heard you tell the head of security, Mr. Duval," he said, looking irritated. The slight accent in his voice gave his words a clipped tone that made them sound rather ominous. Had that been the accent Raul had heard? "Please if I could only speak with you a moment."

"Anything you have to tell me, you can tell Mr. Duval," Pen said, already closing the door on him. He placed his palm against it, his strength easily stopping her. She stared at him, eyes wide. "What are you doing?"

The door to the stairway near his own suite opened and the security officer who was earlier guarding the door appeared. He must have left for only a moment to use the facilities. Gustav had no doubt waited for that moment. The security officer frowned at the scene before him, studying the two of them with mild curiosity.

"Please," Gustav whispered, his hand still on her door.

At this point, Penelope realized she could have protested enough to involve the security officer. On the other hand, if she let Gustav in and he did kill her, he wouldn't have much of an alibi for innocence.

"Is there a problem?" The security officer now seemed even more alert.

Penelope paused, weighing the lessened possibility of danger to herself against her curiosity about what Gustav wanted to discuss.

"No, it's fine," she said, flashing a brief smile at him before opening the door again to let Gustav inside.

"Thank you," he muttered, quickly entering before Pen changed her mind.

She closed the door, but stood near it, ready to quickly

open it once again should things get questionable. "What do you want?"

Gustav eyed the door, no doubt wondering how much the security officer could hear if they remained so close to it. Penelope didn't care and stood her ground, her hand remaining on the doorknob. She carefully studied him. She wasn't too familiar with many Scandinavians, but he had the proper coloring, blond hair and blue eyes. Save for a forehead that was a bit too high and an upper lip that protruded slightly over the bottom lip, he was quite handsome.

"You said you wanted to know what I discussed with the head of security?" Pen pressed.

"I—yes, mostly I wanted to make sure they were certain about the suspect in custody. Did he really kill Miss Adler?"

"No."

"No?" His eyes flashed in surprise.

"Well, they aren't certain about it," Pen conceded. She saw no reason to tell him that it was probably only she who wasn't certain. "Why do you ask?"

"So...they did not discuss anyone else? Any other suspect?"

"Perchance *you*, Mr...?"

He hesitated before answering. "Johansen."

"Mr. Johansen," she said, nodding. "Perhaps you'd better tell me why it is you felt the need to knock on my door at this hour of the night? You were obviously listening while the witnesses gave their statements so you know what happened to Vivian. What are you worried about?"

He grunted out a huff of frustration and grabbed his broad forehead and shook his head. "I'm afraid this was a mistake."

He lurched forward to leave, but Pen had a sudden

change of heart. It was the perfect opportunity to question him, she realized.

"Oh no you don't. You're here now, let's talk."

"No, no, I must—"

"How much did you hear with regard to the murder? The door closing? Did you hear that? Did your sister? I know she was awake when security came to question you, despite what you told security. Was it *your* door that closed?"

His eyes were wide in panic. Pen noted that they had only widened at the mention of his sister.

"What is her name?" She asked in a slightly less demanding tone.

"None of your concern." He lifted his chin which suddenly had a firm set to it.

"I can easily find that out. Is it really such a secret? Vivian was the one to give me your name, by the way. How come she knew yours, but not your sister's? Why was she confined to your cabin during the maiden voyage to New York? Are Scandinavians that protective when it comes to their women?"

"Norwegian," he muttered. "Her name is Elsa. She was...seasick."

"An odd trait for the descendant of the Vikings," Pen said in a wry tone. "What really kept her out of sight? Because from what I saw tonight, she seems to have found her sea legs just fine. You two were certainly having fun."

He blinked as though Pen had struck him. "That is...it is none of your concern."

He tried to get past her again. Pen knew she was no match for his strength if he tried to force his way out of her suite.

"I'll tell the security officer it was your door I heard closing after the shooting."

That was enough to stop him. He looked absurdly wounded as he stared at Penelope. "That is a lie."

She couldn't help a sharp laugh, and instantly regretted it when the hurt look on his face deepened. "I don't want to lie, Gustav. I want the truth."

He didn't answer, but he no longer tried to escape either.

"Is your sister in some kind of trouble?"

Pen studied his reaction. The dear boy was particularly guileless she noted, wearing his emotions right on his face. There was a quick look of panic before he forced a mask of neutrality back down.

"Why would you think she is in trouble?"

"Why would you keep her locked away in her room on the way to New York?"

Again, he looked perplexed. "I did not. She was..."

"Sick, yes, you said," Penelope's voice dripped with sarcasm. She quickly tried to piece it all together.

Elsa was confined to her room on the maiden voyage to New York, no one getting a good look at her...save for perhaps the maid servicing their suite?

"Did you know Marie Blanchet?"

"Marie Blanchet?" The ignorance in his expression seemed credible.

"The maid who serviced your room on the way to New York? She went missing the final night. Would Elsa know anything about that? Was she upset that a member of the crew managed to get a good look at her?"

"What are you saying?" He studied her with concern.

"I'm saying that it's odd your sister spent ten days locked

in her room, such that no one got a good look at her save for the maid who serviced that room. And Vivian, by the way. She saw enough to notice your sister had filled out her dress a bit more last night." Pen gasped. "Is she...with child?"

His face reddened so fast, it might as well have been a traffic light. "Of course not!"

"I could see how that is something you'd want to keep to yourself. I have no intention of telling anyone. But it does create a problem if that is a secret you'd be willing to kill for. The two people who may have discovered it are now dead."

A look of horror came to his face. "Why would either of us do such a thing? What you said is not the truth."

Penelope shook her head in frustration. Either Gustav was a much better liar than she gave him credit for or she was following utterly the wrong path.

She put up a hand, giving herself a moment. "Let me work this out now, while I have you. Elsa is supposedly seasick the entire voyage to New York, such that she remains confined to her room. You two spend only ten days in New York despite the equally long voyage to get there, doubled when coming back. And that doesn't even include the travel from Norway to the South of France—yet another puzzling element to all of this." She studied him, but he had managed to settle his face into the picture of neutrality by then. "She is bundled up like a present on Christmas Eve when boarding the ship, but once on board, she feels perfectly at ease to attend a party in full view of everyone."

Gustav remained impassive, giving nothing away now.

"What happened in New York?"

His gaze cooled as he assessed her. "I see now that you know nothing, Miss Banks. I apologize for intruding upon you. Please excuse me."

This time there was no stopping him. He barged right

past her and took hold of the door, swinging it open and her along with it.

"My apologies," He said, oddly enough looking truly apologetic for practically manhandling her. In a softer tone, low enough that the security officer wouldn't hear him. "I promise, she did not kill either woman. But I must protect her."

Penelope stared after him as he strode right past the security guard scrutinizing him, and opened the door to his suite. He closed it shut behind him.

It caused Penelope to flinch in surprise. But it wasn't the loudness of it that caused her to stare perfectly stunned at the door right across the short hallway from her. It was the realization that it was most certainly not the same sound she'd heard after Vivian's murder. The door to the Johansens' suite wasn't the door that she'd heard closing after Vivian's murder.

CHAPTER FOURTEEN

SLEEP DID MANAGE TO CREEP PAST PENELOPE'S defenses, long enough to carry her well into the morning. By the time she woke up, the sun was almost at the midpoint in the sky. The events of the evening—thankfully not too tainted by an overindulgence of legal alcohol—played back in her head like a colorized motion picture.

The opening scene took place at the bar, sitting with Vivian as she named all the passengers who were on the maiden voyage. The final scene cut to Gustav closing the door behind him, and Penelope realizing that it hadn't been his door she'd heard right after Vivian's murder.

That was enough to have her quickly getting out of bed. Penelope dismissed the usual routine of incurring the services of a maid to get herself ready. Most of her peers would probably be appalled that she wasn't traveling with a personal maid of her own. Three years of suffering the "indignity" of pulling her own outfits from the closet and dressing herself had made such trappings of the wealthy seem unnecessary, frivolous even. No, it was far more efficient to dress oneself if only to get on with the day.

121

Half an hour later, she was quite presentable in a dress with a carnation pink top and navy blue pleated skirt and matching blue loose bowtie. She wasn't surprised to find Richard and Cousin Cordelia already up and about somewhere on the ship. Lulu and Benny were notorious night owls though. She tried the former first. Pen adored Benny and was often amused by his wicked sense of humor, but she wanted a more sensible head that morning.

"Lulu, it's Pen," she said as she knocked. Her friend opened the door, wearing a white silk robe and her hair still pinned and wrapped.

"Come on in," she said with a tired smile.

Pen entered and closed the door behind her.

"I'm guessing you're not done with your sleuthing, though I don't know how *I'm* supposed to help you," Lulu said, gracefully falling back into the couch and crossing her legs. The color of the Pearl Suite, beautifully decorated in white with gold fixtures, almost matched her robe, and attractively contrasted with her brown skin.

Pen remained standing, pacing as she spoke. "Of course I'm sleuthing," she said, dismissively waving a hand. "I had a visit from Gustav last night."

"You what?" Lulu sat up straighter and pinned Penelope in place with just a look. "And what did he have to say for himself? Or that *supposed* sister of his."

"How do you mean?" Pen said, studying Lulu with bewilderment.

"Ah, I see it now." A smile of understanding came to Lulu's face. "You don't have brothers or sisters. Well, I do, one of each. And let me tell you something, those two ain't brother and sister, honey."

Penelope wrinkled her brow, replaying what she saw of

Gustav and Elsa at the bar, then prior to that at the pier. "They're just close, is all."

Lulu laughed. "And Benny is just waiting for the right gal to come along, like your poor Cousin Cordelia still believes for some reason."

Pen put her hand on her hip and gave Lulu a skeptical look. "Why would they pretend to be siblings?"

"You tell me, Miss Lady Detective."

Pen frowned in thought. This was exactly why she had come to Lulu. She always had some nugget of relevant wisdom to plop right into her hand without adorning it in flair or warnings or histrionics like Benny, Richard, or Cousin Cordelia would. Penelope had heard Lulu mention a sister a few times, and her brother even less, but she'd always kept that part of her life firmly on one side of a wall she'd built up between that and the life she shared with Pen.

Penelope didn't have siblings, though she'd certainly seen many among her friends. Some of them bickered incessantly, others got along smashingly. But did they dance with each other, giggle conspiratorially, escape to secluded sections of a bar, share a suite with...

"Oh!" Pen suddenly exclaimed. "If their suite matches mine, there is only one bedroom."

Lulu simply arched an eyebrow.

"But it could still be twin beds. Plenty of siblings grew up sharing a room."

"And as adults, ones who could afford these fine First Class accommodations? Why would they?"

Pen nibbled her thumb in thought. "Yes, they are hiding something, but...I don't think it's murder—at least not Vivian's."

"How do you figure that?"

"Help me out with an experiment," Pen exclaimed, running toward the door.

"Can I at least get dressed first?"

"It's just in the hallway. No one is paying attention to you."

"To *you*, maybe. But Miss Lucille Simmons will be getting dressed."

Pen was impatient, but she didn't argue. Lucille often had to remind her that they experienced two different worlds and thus, had to act accordingly. While she waited, she bounced on her feet, mulling over everything Lulu had just said.

If Gustav and Elsa weren't siblings, what were they? The most obvious answer was that they were secretly lovers. But why would that be such a scandal? Why pretend to be siblings? And why did Elsa hide from view on the way to New York, but feel free to reveal herself on the way back, and then only once on the ship? What had happened while they were in America? Had they finally gotten married? But why go all the way to America to do that?

When Lulu appeared again, she looked fabulous as always in a gray silk dress with lapis blue embellishments. Yet another mystery surrounding her friend. Pen had known Lulu long enough to surmise she came from her own bit of money, but even that didn't account for how extraordinarily fashionable she always was. Now certainly wasn't the time to delve into that, not that she'd get much more than the usual vague answer to her prying.

"So, what are we doing, detective?" Lulu asked with a smirk.

"Testing doors." She ignored the puzzled look on Lulu's face as she took her hand and hurried her out into the hallway. "I'm going to stand by my door, leaving it open only partially while you exit into the stairwell across the way. Pretend you just shot someone and are escaping."

After giving Pen a bemused look, Lulu strutted over to the stairwell. Pen opened her own door and stepped inside the suite. She took hold of the knob and opened it just a bit. When Lulu exited, in a slight rush, she listened carefully.

"Well?" Lulu said, coming right back out to join Pen who stepped out to meet her. "Was that the door you heard?"

"I'm almost certain of it."

"That means it could have been anyone."

"Yes, it certainly does." Penelope tested her own door just to be sure. It was too loud, no matter how she closed it, to be the door she'd heard the night before. "I suppose it makes sense for the door to the stairwell to be more muted. No need to annoy the passengers in cabins nearby every time someone exits."

"Maybe it's this mysterious man Cousin Cordelia saw?"

"Who could easily be a passenger, or a woman for that matter. Raul said he couldn't exactly tell. If they knew he was in the suite, they might have masked their real voice, knowing he couldn't see them at the time of the shooting."

Lulu laughed softly and shook her head. "Aren't detectives supposed to be narrowing down suspects?"

"You'd think limiting it to a boat would make it easier."

"Well, well, well, look who has finally decided to make use of the day."

They both turned to see Benny, arm in arm with Cousin Cordelia.

"Benny was kind enough to join me in a pre-lunch game of bridge. I needed something to take my mind off that awful business last night." Cousin Cordelia's eyes flicked past Pen to Vivian's door, then closed with dismay before returning to her. She patted Benny's hand. "He's such a dear. Didn't want to wake either of you, but was happy to accommodate an old widow."

"Now, now," Benny said, patting her hand right back. "Bridge happens to be one of my favorite pastimes. And with such a maestra as you for my partner, it was the cat's meow, dove." He shot Pen a conspiratorial smile. "And it was the most wonderful marketplace of gossip. You two will never guess what interesting little trinket of information we stumbled upon."

CHAPTER FIFTEEN

PENELOPE SCRUTINIZED BENNY. "HOW MUCH GOSSIP could you have possibly picked up over the course of a morning? Has news spread about Vivian so quickly?"

"Of course it has, Pen. You saw how many curious eyes were crowded in the hallways last night. Tongues have been wagging, dove, each one speculating as to who is the guilty party. Naturally, after last night's dinner, the most obvious suspect is Simone—after Raul, of course."

"I certainly hope you didn't pay too much for that rather obvious tidbit in your *marketplace of gossip*," Pen said in a sardonic tone.

Benny pursed his lips at Pen, as though she should be ashamed for even suggesting that was all he had.

"We really shouldn't be gossiping so," Cousin Cordelia admonished, looking around. She added in a more discreet tone, "It is so very vulgar."

That was rather ironic, being that Cousin Cordelia was second only to Benny when it came to devouring gossip, the more sordid the better. However, Pen's cousin prided propriety above even that, so she graciously gestured toward her suite to give them a few walls and a door for privacy.

"I take it you didn't happen upon Richard while you were playing cards?"

"We weren't *playing cards*, Penelope," Cousin Cordelia said, filled with umbrage. "We were playing bridge."

"My apologies," Pen said, giving a conspiratorial smile to Benny and Lulu.

"However, no," Cousin Cordelia continued. She gave Pen a skeptical look. "Though, he doesn't strike me as a bridge player."

"No, he isn't. He must be getting some fresh sea air," Penelope said in a breezy voice, ignoring the looks the others were giving her and then each other. They had probably sensed the tension between Richard and herself lately, but were being tactful about it.

"Now then," Benny said, looking rather prim as he sat on the edge of the sofa. Lulu and Cousin Cordelia sat on either side of him. Pen remained standing. "Since you so handily dismissed Simone as the suspect—"

"I'm almost certain Simone was in her room," Pen interjected. "Lulu and I just performed a test. It was most definitely the door to the stairwell that I heard last night. She couldn't have gone into the stairwell and then back to her own room in the time it took for me to open the door and see what the popping noise I'd heard was."

"She could have opened that door as a ploy, then more quietly entered her own room?" Cousin Cordelia suggested.

"Cousin, what a devious mind you have," Pen said with admiration.

Her cousin scoffed, tilting her chin up. "I most certainly do not. It's just that I *have* read one or two detective novels,

Penelope. I've learned there are no limits one will stoop to in order to cover up a crime."

Cousin Cordelia's suggestion was unlikely, but not entirely implausible. It was best to explore all avenues. Simone would have known she'd be the most likely suspect, so it made sense for her to cover her tracks as much as possible.

"What is this gossip you heard?" Pen said, turning to Benny.

"Ah yes," he said, pleased to be the center of attention once again. "That prissy little man, Gerard, you know the Master of Ceremonies, or however he fancies himself. Well, it seems he is in a bit of hot water. Some hubbub surrounding this horrid murder."

"They think *he's* responsible for Vivian's death?"

"Not directly."

Pen narrowed her gaze. "What *exactly* did this fountain of gossip impart to you? No need to embellish," she added as a warning.

He briefly frowned at her, then proceeded. "We were playing with the most darling little widow who is actually from Nottingham, if you can believe it. Her name is Hazel, and she's taken her dearly departed husband's money and has decided to travel the world. She wants to feel young again. How precious is that? She's been touring the U.S. visiting all the interesting sites, particularly the Wild West. She took a train just to see the O.K. Corral—the very idea! Then there was the Grand Canyon and the Alamo and—"

"Benny!" Pen said. "No embellishment."

He stuck his bottom lip out, but sighed and continued. "My point *is...*" he said, glaring at Pen. "...she *wasn't* on the maiden voyage. However, she's such a delight, she just has a way of talking to people, more importantly, getting them to talk to her. Well, a member of the cleaning staff, Léa, was spiffing up the library this morning, she happens to be just as loquacious as our darling Brit, Hazel. She all but told her that *Monsieur Canard* was escorted from the morning staff briefing by Alfred and *two* members of the security staff. She told Hazel that if it wasn't for the rumors that would have ensued, he most definitely would have been in handcuffs."

Pen remembered the name of the maid. Léa was the one who had been pressing Elise for information about Vivian, suggesting that perhaps she had been the one to murder Marie. She knew a mischief-maker when she saw one, and Léa was guilty as charged.

Still, *three* members of security coming to escort Gerard away, and in front of the staff? Whatever they had learned about him must have been urgent to be that tactless.

"We did have to rescue poor Vivian from him last night." Benny pointed out, realizing he had captured Pen's interest. "I just assumed he was a harmless toady, but perhaps there is something more sinister about the fellow?"

"And he does have nearly white hair and access to the staff tuxedos," Pen said in thought. The lighting in the hallway could have made his hair seem blonde under the top hat. She looked at Cousin Cordelia. "Could it have been him you saw at Vivian's door?"

"Oh, Penelope, it was so far away and, as I stated, he had his back turned to me."

"Why don't we narrow down the possible list of suspects to start?" Penelope said. "Raul hearing the killer mention a maid, it makes me think perhaps Vivian discovered who Marie's killer was last night."

"So anyone blonde, or with light hair, who was on the maiden voyage," Benny said. "That's a fair number of people, even when limited to passengers. Though, in the case of Simone, all one has to do is look at those eyebrows to know her blonde hair is bought and paid for."

"Well, she's presently blonde so she gets included. Would she have a tuxedo though?" Pen asked with a frown.

"You'd be surprised what a determined person is capable of," Lulu said. "I doubt the uniforms for the staff are kept in a vault."

Pen nodded in concession. "So to begin with, we have Gerard, who has suddenly risen higher on the list now. We need to know why he was taken by security this morning. Surely, if they thought he was guilty of killing Vivian, they would release Raul."

"Unless they decided it was easier to simply place the blame on him," Lulu suggested.

Pen considered that. "It can't be good publicity to have a member of the crew be a victim of murder and then another accused of murder. Particularly when the French lines are still so new to the industry. Still, I don't want to accuse them of covering up for murder until we know more. Let's move on to other candidates."

"Well, there's your Norwegian fella and his...*gal*," Lulu said with a smirk. Benny, another only child, turned to scrutinize Lulu in confusion.

"Lulu seems to think those two aren't really brother and sister as they claim. He came to visit me this morning, and insisted they had nothing to hide. What do you say, Benny? Did they look more like kissing cousins last night?"

He seemed to consider it. "They were awfully friendly with one another. I can believe it. But why pose as his sister?"

"That's a good question, among many." Pen thought about the night before. "I wish I'd seen if he came out of his room or from somewhere else. It might make him a more likely suspect."

"Where was his sister?" Lulu asked. "Everyone and their brother—so to speak—was out of their rooms last night sticking their nose in this murder. Did anyone see her?"

Pen was surprised she hadn't considered that herself. "I saw him talk to someone in his room, but that could have been a ploy. He claimed his sister was still sleeping through it all. What if she wasn't even there as Lulu suggested? What if she was the one to escape into the stairwell?"

"That would mean whatever this secret of theirs is, it's enough to kill for," Cousin Cordelia said, looking ravenous with interest.

"People kill for the silliest reasons, unfortunately. One person wouldn't kill even to protect themselves, whereas another would kill over nothing more than a dirty look."

"But to plan it so meticulously, to the point she'd dress in her brother's tuxedo and top hat, come back even when thwarted by your cousin, then sit in wait in Vivian's room for the perfect opportunity to shoot her?" Benny asked. "And where did she get the gun?"

"Ten days in America is certainly enough time to get one," Lulu said in a wry tone.

"Which can be said of every one of our other suspects. Though, that would lean in favor of a passenger being the guilty party, as the crew were forced to remain on board while in New York. Speaking of which, there is still Edwin and his father to consider," Pen said. "His father, at least, definitely has something to hide. Why keep his son from socializing?"

"Are we sure it wasn't just Vivian he was keeping Edwin from?" Benny asked.

"Frankly, there are a lot of questions surrounding their

trip. The same ones I have for our Norwegian couple. Why would any of them go all the way to the South of France to board a ship to the United States? And why stay only ten days? As for Edwin, we know his father kept him in Long Island, well out of the city. Why?"

"He did just turn eighteen. Perhaps this was a birthday trip?" Benny suggested.

"He didn't seem all that happy with it," Pen replied.

"Don't you think perhaps Richard should be involved in this?" Cousin Cordelia asked. "I know he wouldn't want you going after a murderer on your own Penelope, dear."

"I'm not alone," Pen said, giving a satisfied smile to Lulu and Benny. "And Kitty is somewhere on this boat, meddling far more than I am. In fact, we should find her and see what she's managed to discover."

"Must we?" Benny said with a sigh.

"It's about time for lunch, and I'm perfectly famished. Perhaps she's in the café."

Perhaps Richard is as well, Pen thought to herself, not wanting to state that out loud. So much for their plans to finally have a space to themselves and convenient proximity to one another. Though, murder did tend to dim the candle of romance.

"Let's go," she said in a snap. "Either Kitty or Richard is bound to have discovered something."

CHAPTER SIXTEEN

PENELOPE, BENNY, LULU, AND COUSIN CORDELIA
went to the café on board the ship. It was a more casual
affair than the dining room, made to look like a typical street
café in France, with braided wicker chairs and small intimate tables. The large widows revealing so much of the
bright blue sky made it feel as though one was sitting
outdoors on a Parisian street underneath an awning. It
presented a cheerful ambiance that almost took one's mind
off the fact that someone had been murdered the night
prior.

It was odd that the ship hadn't put out a statement yet.
Perhaps they were waiting to make sure they had the right
suspect in custody. That was good for Raul's sake. Still, the
longer they waited, the more the rumor mill would spin.

Which it most definitely had if the café was any indication. The news had infused the air with a sense of unease.
Rather than the sound of happy chatting, passengers spoke
in hushed tones. Rather than expressions of relaxed pleasure, there were frowns and creased brows. Backs were rigid

like frightened prey ready to flee. Eyes were wide and darting, suspecting every passenger around them.

Penelope's motley little crew earned a good dose of that suspicion as they walked in. She could hear the murmured whispers grow louder and more fervent. Every eye was pinned on them as they stood at the entrance in search of a group of tables to occupy.

And there was Katherine Andrews.

No gaze was quite as piercing as that of Kitty's as she stared back at them. She arched a brow when Penelope met her eyes, as though daring her to sit elsewhere. Pen flashed a smile and led the others over to her table.

Kitty had at least been sensible enough to choose a location furthest away from the other passengers. The glimmer that came to her eyes meant she had something scandalous to impart.

"Sit, sit!" Kitty said, her lips pursed with pleasure as she gestured to everyone, reserving a taunting glare for Benny.

"I take it you've learned something related to last night's murder?" Pen asked.

"I most certainly have, all while the rest of you were sleeping in or galavanting around the ship," she said, twirling a hand in the air. "But of course, I'm a journalist and it's my duty to report on serious matters. The public has a right to know these things, and I'm not one to rest on my laurels."

Benny shot her a patronizing look as he clapped. "Brava, Kitty, whatever would the world do without your nose for reporting?"

"Well, they certainly wouldn't know that a gun was stolen from the security office below deck."

"*What?*" Pen wasn't the only one to exclaim in surprise.

She winced and looked around to find all eyes on their section of the café once again. In a quieter voice she added, "How do you know this?"

Before Kitty could answer, a waiter came by to take their food orders from the à la carte menu. Pen recognized him as one of the young men carrying champagne bottles for the departure party. For the café, he wore more casual attire that befitted the Parisian café aesthetic. The sleeves of his white shirt were rolled up and he sported a black tuxedo vest and black tie. His black pants were mostly hidden by the long white apron wrapped around his lower half.

The staff really did make full use of each part of the tuxedo. That meant that perhaps there was a full supply of them somewhere in rotation between cleanings. With the news that the gun used in Vivian's murder may have been stolen from the downstairs security office, Pen now had to widen her net of suspects to include the crew and staff. Fortunately for him, their waiter had dark hair.

That's at least one suspect I can eliminate. Hopefully, blondes weren't quite as common below deck.

Penelope quickly gave her order along with everyone else, then turned her attention back to Kitty. She happily kept everyone waiting with bated breath under the guise of making sure the waiter was well out of earshot.

"As you might imagine, it's been much more difficult to gain access to the staff and crew since poor Vivian's...*murder*," she added in a whisper. "Other than in the ordinary course of their assigned duties, the staff and crew are *strictly* forbidden from speaking with the passengers. Still, I'm nothing if not resourceful."

They all ignored a soft snort from Benny.

Kitty continued, undeterred. "I became the most

demanding passenger on the ship, constantly requesting items be brought to my cabin, continuously getting lost below deck, wandering haplessly into places I shouldn't be without realizing it, trapping poor waiters, waitresses, and bartenders into conversations."

"I'm sure they loved you for that."

"One does what one must for the sake of the truth, Pen," Kitty scoffed. "Don't you think they also want to see justice done and the murderer found?"

"Perhaps you could kindly tell us *how* you came about this information? Who was it that told you?" Penelope asked.

"My journalistic integrity prohibits me from revealing my sources."

"*Kitty*," Pen uttered in exasperation.

She shrugged. "But trust that it is true. Surely you can use this information to help your dear Raul?" She batted her eyelashes at Pen.

"He's not my dear anything," Pen retorted. Still, she considered what Kitty had said. Kitty liked to glorify herself a bit, and enjoyed rolling around in the muck of good dirt, but she wasn't known to be an outright liar, especially about something as serious as murder. "Can you at least tell me how your source knows?"

Kitty considered it, then nodded. "She is, *ahem*, rather close with a member of the security team, if you know what I mean."

"I can hazard a guess," Pen said dryly.

"Really, the entire below-stairs area is a perfect bacchanal," Kitty continued gleefully. "You know what they say about close proximity. It's enough to make Dionysus blush. They are all fairly young and attractive, so who could blame them?"

Cousin Cordelia squeaked out a brief sound of shock.

"And she just offered this information to you without prompting?" Pen was skeptical.

"Well, I may have *paid* her."

"Journalistic integrity, hmm?" Benny said with a snort.

"Do you think this has anything to do with Gerard's being taken away?" Lulu asked, always the sensible one bringing everyone back to the primary concern.

"Gerard? That pretentious little man? What about him?"

"You aren't the only *resourceful* one on board, Kitty," Benny gloated. "I discovered the man was practically taken away in handcuffs right in front of most of the staff."

"For reasons we don't know," Pen quickly added.

"I can't imagine someone like him committing murder," Cousin Cordelia said. "He seems so proper and sophisticated."

"He's a simpering fool," Kitty said. "Obviously upset that Vivian snubbed him last night."

"That's hardly cause for murder."

"He's also the one who spent the most time with Marie Blanchet, being her boss and all," Lulu pointed out. "Perhaps she knew something about him and was as loosey-goosey with the dirt as Kitty's source is. Maybe Marie told Vivian, and she accidentally let it slip last night while talking to Gerard."

"That might explain why we haven't seen his toadying presence lingering," Benny said.

"It is a persuasive theory," Pen said thoughtfully. Suddenly, an idea came to her and she sat up straighter. "I know exactly how to find out, without Kitty having to reveal her source," she added giving her a twist of the lips.

"How?" Kitty asked, her eyes narrowed with skepticism.

"I'm going to confess to everyone in the security office," Penelope replied, springing from her seat even as the waiter was bringing their food. Pen had a rather more urgent hunger to satisfy.

CHAPTER SEVENTEEN

PEN HAD REACHED THE PUBLIC-FACING SECURITY office. It had the same Art Deco aesthetic as the rest of the passenger part of the ship, with patterned carpet and a long sleek black desk behind which sat two security officers.

The one with the name badge that read, Jules, had a pleasant face that seemed permanently settled into something amiable. The other, Marcel, was almost his opposite with a neck matching the size of his head and a mouth that had a downward set to it. It turned into a full frown when he saw Penelope enter. She recognized his face as one that was in her hallway last night, urging passengers back into their rooms.

"My name is Penelope Banks, and I need to speak to Monsieur Duval. It's about Vivian Adler's murder."

That had both their brows rising with sudden interest. They eyed each other, determining who would speak first. Marcel was the one who eventually did.

"Do you have more information to provide?" He seemed quite interested in being the first to know.

"I'm afraid it is a matter that I must discuss directly with

Monsieur Duval," she said, adding a tinge of haughtiness to her voice and expression. Pen rarely put on such airs, but it usually served its purpose. In order for this to work, it had to be done just right.

He sighed and picked up the phone. Most likely because of the airs she'd put on, he spoke barely audible in French. She did hear her name mentioned, and it wasn't a surprise when she saw him nod before hanging up.

"Monsieur Duval will be up shortly."

Penelope paused before speaking up again. "I know I should wait for Monsieur Duval," she began, pausing just long enough to pique their interest before continuing, "but I should confess...I know the gun used in Vivian's murder was stolen from the security office."

As expected, that got an instant physical reaction from both of them. They practically rose from their seats with alarm.

Pen continued before they could speak. "I only know because a member of your security team happened to confide in another member of staff, who then told a friend of mine."

She studied them closely. Jules looked aghast, as though he couldn't imagine one of his fellow security officers doing such a thing. Marcel's expression bordered on disgust.

So, it hadn't been either of them. It would have been much easier if it had been.

Penelope sighed and shook her head, showing agreement with their disapproval.

"I demand to know who this member of staff is that told your friend," Marcel said, his fist pounding on the desk.

"I'm certain Monsieur Duval would prefer to have that information first," she hinted. His face reddened, but he didn't ask again.

When Alfred arrived, Pen acted quickly. She took his arm and gently guided him back out of the office and further down the hall before either member of his team could repeat what she had said.

"Monsieur Duval, I have a rather important request."

"A request?" He frowned, as though annoyed she had wasted his time when there was more urgent business at hand.

"I must speak to you and every member of your team someplace privately. Naturally, I realize you must keep two men in the public office in case of an emergency, but the rest should be present."

"Is this related to Vivian's murder?"

"It may be."

"Then you should tell me. *I* will be the one to tell my staff, Mademoiselle Banks."

Penelope considered the man she was addressing and tried a different tactic than that she had used with Marcel. An ingratiating smile came to her face and a pleading look colored her eyes.

"Of course Monsieur Duval. It isn't that I don't trust you, it's just that...well, this is a *very* important bit of information and I think it's critical they all hear it at the same time and directly from me. It's...a confession."

"A confession?" He scrutinized her, no doubt wondering if she was pulling some prank.

"Yes."

"Why should they all need to hear it?"

"Because it may affect one of them and I need to know which one."

"If this is some ploy, some attempt to conduct your own investigation, then—"

"I'm simply saving us both time. It should only take five minutes, if that. Trust me, it will be for your benefit as well."

He considered it, then sighed and pinched the bridge of his nose. Pen would have felt bad if she didn't think the end result would be worth it. With an irritable grunt, he continued on, urging Pen to follow him. She breathed a sigh of relief.

Once again she followed him down below. They wound their way through the corridors until they reached the security office. There were two men there, as before, Jean and David. Alfred ordered David to retrieve Alain and Joseph—who apparently rounded out the total of the security team—and bring them back.

Penelope's eyes darted to the holding cell.

Alfred noticed it and answered her unspoken question. "Oui, Monsieur García is still there."

"May I speak with him again?" At the very least it would keep Alfred from asking questions of her or prying before she had a chance to conduct her little experiment.

Alfred's eyes narrowed with suspicion, wondering if it was wise to allow it. "I will see if he is willing."

He walked over and opened the window, then curtly asked if Raul would be willing to speak with her. She heard his voice eagerly reply that he would. Pen figured a night alone in a cell might make anyone want to speak with another human being.

Alfred opened the door for her and she walked in. She was surprised to find him freshly bathed and wearing a change of clothing. It seemed the French weren't draconian in their treatment of prisoners. Perhaps Monsieur Duval wasn't entirely certain he had the right suspect?

"How are you, Raul?"

"*Bien*, good, now that I see you. Have you learned anything?" There was a hopeful look in his eyes.

"I have some theories on what may have happened." Best to be vague in front of Alfred.

Raul gave Pen a weak smile, it faltered and his gaze lowered before rising again to meet hers. "I am sorry, Penelope. I know it was wrong of me to use the painting that way. If I had not gone to America to sell it in the first place, perhaps...." A bitter twist came to his mouth.

"No need for regrets now, Raul. This will all work itself out. Can you tell me what you and Vivian discussed while you were painting her?"

"You, mostly."

"Really?" Pen was taken aback by that.

He shrugged and one side of his mouth cocked up. "You and that *Richard* of yours, but mostly you. She wanted to know more about you and your investigation business. She was fascinated by a woman in such a career. Unfortunately, I had nothing to tell her, as I was not aware of what you do. I am not surprised though," he said, grinning at her. "It is a perfect job for you, Penelope. You were always finding things I had misplaced."

"Don't tell me you spent the entire time talking about me."

"I was not there for long. I did not get to paint very much before she grew tired and wanted to go to bed."

"Of course." It had been a rather late night for all of them.

A wan smile appeared again and he tilted his head to study her. "I think about you often, the time we had together. It seemed simpler then—easier." Something tragic filled his eyes before he sighed and he fell back against the wall.

"The past always seems simpler," Pen said. She wouldn't forget what had led her to Spain in the first place. There was nothing simple or easy about losing her beloved mother.

She wanted to ask him about Clifford, anything he could tell her that might give her an indication as to why her ex-fiancé wanted this painting of her. The thought still sent a shiver of revulsion up her spine. Hadn't he humiliated her enough?

David returned with Alain and Joseph, cutting short the brief reunion. Penelope left Raul with an encouraging smile. Alfred closed the door to the cell behind her.

It was a crowded affair in the office, with the four officers, Alfred, and Penelope. But at least it gave her a moment to study each of them and note their names.

"Now then, Mademoiselle Banks, what is it you have to say? You mentioned it would be brief," Alfred added as a warning.

"Yes, of course." She took a breath and once again scanned the faces before her, all of which looked on with various degrees of curiosity. "I know the gun used to murder Vivian Adler was taken from this office. I know because a member of this security office told another crew member who then told a friend of mine."

The reaction was instant, mostly in angry French. It was first directed at Penelope, then each other as they shot accusatory glances around the small room.

Alfred was the one to settle them with nothing more than a loud bark. He turned to Penelope, his expression filled with anger. "Mademoiselle Banks, that is a very serious accusation, and highly inappropriate for you to be spreading about."

"I'm not the one spreading it about, as I just indicated.

As I stated, I only heard it third-hand, which means every passenger on the ship will probably know by dinner tonight."

He blustered for a bit, but before he could respond, the phone in the office rang. Alfred exhaled with exasperation, then jerked his chin at one of his team to answer it while he dealt with Penelope.

"This is a matter for security, and security only. I strongly caution you against spreading this dangerous information, Mademoiselle Banks."

"Of course I won't," Pen said, her eyes lowered with demure lament. Her ears, on the other hand, were perked, listening to the one side of the phone conversation she could hear, as the man who had answered it suddenly became agitated.

"Calm down, I don't understand. You say you found who?" The man spoke in fervent French. There was a pause before he continued, even more agitated. *"Her body?"*

That had everyone in the room, including Alfred instantly diverting their attention to the phone conversation. Pen took on an expression of confused curiosity, pretending not to understand the French being spoken. She figured it might serve her well in her investigation, the way it had with Elise and Léa.

"Marie Blanchet, you say. Impossible! She is—" There was a pause. By now, each of his fellow officers crowded him, trying to listen in. He had to quiet the burst of excited and puzzled exclamations that arose at his statement.

Even Penelope could barely contain her rabid curiosity. They'd found Marie's body? Hadn't they performed a search of the ship when she'd first been reported missing? How had she suddenly been found again?

"*Let me have that*," Alfred interjected, snatching the phone out of his hands. "*Marcel? Repeat everything.*"

Pen watched his stern expression gradually transition to one of horror. "*Yes, I will be right up.*"

He hung up the phone and took a moment, staring hard at the floor in thought before straightening up. He seemed to realize Pen was still in the room and a look of extreme consternation came to his face.

"Joseph, please escort Mademoiselle Banks back to the passenger levels," he said in English, his eyes boring into her as he tried to determine how much she had heard and understood.

"Was that something about Marie Blanchet? I heard you mention her name. Is there news about what happened to her?" Pen asked, her eyes wide with dimwitted curiosity.

"That is none of your concern." He relaxed a bit at her apparent ignorance, assuming she hadn't understood the French spoken. He nodded to Joseph. "Please take her."

Penelope obliged without argument, following Joseph out. As she left, she considered everything she had suddenly learned. The news about Marie was certainly a wild card she hadn't expected in this investigation.

She smiled at Joseph's back, realizing that she had a trump card of her own. She had carefully studied the faces of the men when she had revealed she knew about the gun. Anyone paying attention, and she certainly had been, would have seen the brief, ashen look of guilt on the face of one man in particular.

CHAPTER EIGHTEEN

PENELOPE WAS PARTICULARLY FAMISHED BY THE TIME Joseph had planted her firmly on the First Class deck, but she hesitated going back to the café. She wanted a moment to process the news about Marie, so she headed back to her suite instead. The only thing she knew, based on what she had heard from one side of the phone conversation, was that they had found her body.

Was Marie's body on the ship? Or had she been found floating in the ocean?

In either circumstance, after nearly two weeks, her body had to be in an unfortunate state. In the ocean, there would be little left after the fish had gotten to her. On the ship, the smell alone would have alerted someone long before now. Perhaps she had been in cold storage somewhere?

Unless...

"She was only recently murdered!"

Had Marie been alive this whole time? If so, where had she been? Where could she have hidden that they wouldn't find her?

"Someone on the crew helped hide her," Pen whispered to herself.

No wonder Alfred had looked so upset.

When she arrived to the floor where her suite was, she was surprised to see Richard in the hallway, just leaving his suite.

"Where have you been?" Pen asked, momentarily setting aside the news about Marie.

She couldn't help but notice the quick flash of guilt on his face before he gave her an easy smile. Perhaps it was just her imagination. "You weren't up by breakfast so I've been enjoying a few of the ship's amenities on my own. There's a small gym on board. I went there for an hour or so. Then, after washing up, I checked out some books from the library. Otherwise, I've just been wandering and exploring."

Penelope studied him for a moment, then sighed, too exhausted to be suspicious. Besides, she had other priorities.

"Have you even eaten yet?" Richard asked, a concerned look on his face as he studied her. "You look rather drawn."

"Well thank you for that," she snapped, much harsher than intended.

He didn't so much as wince. "Come on, let's get something inside of you."

"I don't want to eat," she grumbled, her hunger making her more irritable. "There's too much going on."

"Like what?" He asked cautiously, already knowing it was related to Vivian's murder.

"The gun that was used was taken from the security office. Kitty heard it from a member of the staff—she won't reveal the name—who heard it from a member of the security team."

"So that's where it came from." He didn't seem all that surprised.

"Also, they found Marie Blanchet's body."

"*What?*"

Pen felt only a brief bit of satisfaction that she had managed to stun him. There was no joy in being irritated with or getting the better of Richard. She *had* slept in late, after all. She couldn't very well have expected him to wait until noon to start his own day with her. And there *were* many amenities on board where one could pass the time out of sight.

"I was in the security office below deck and—"

"Why?" He frowned.

"I wanted to see who the officer was that divulged the information to a fellow member of staff who then told Kitty."

Richard sighed and grabbed the back of his neck. "I assume you found out, and there is a reason *why* you went to so much trouble to do just that."

"If you're asking if I still think Raul is innocent, yes I do. It's beyond just the painting by now. I don't know how many different ways to tell you I don't have feelings for him, Richard. I just—I don't think he did it." Richard only seemed half-appeased. "In all fairness, the phone call about Marie came in while I was down there."

"Right," he said in thought, mentally shifting his focus. "That is quite the coincidence."

"Not really. We always assumed they were connected. Whoever killed Vivian also then killed Marie."

"So it was after Vivian's murder?"

"I'm not sure."

"I assume you have some scheme to learn more?"

"I do."

"But before we do anything, you need to eat, Penelope."

"Yes, I do," she admitted, feeling lightheaded at the reminder. There was no point in denying it any longer.

"Come on, let's go to the café. We can discuss this there."

"Oh," she said with some dismay, "all the others are probably still there. Alfred cautioned me against telling anyone about any of this."

"I'm sure he did," Richard said with a short laugh, as he continued leading her to the elevator.

"Naturally, they know about the gun, but not about Marie. Oh, and there's more! Gustav paid me a short visit this morning."

"What?" Richard stopped and turned to her, anger blazing in his eyes. "What did he do to you?"

Pen smiled at his overprotectiveness. "Don't worry, he wasn't dangerous." She told him about Gustav's questions and concerns, then about Lulu's suggestion that they weren't really siblings.

"Well, I'm hardly one to be a good judge of close siblings," Richard said, having a tenuous relationship with his own brother. "But I can see how that might be true. So, why pretend?"

"My thoughts exactly. Something must have happened either in New York or on the way there. At least now we know Marie wasn't murdered back then. If her body was found on board, she would have been in hiding somewhere on the ship. Now the theory that the person who killed her was someone who was both on the maiden voyage and the return trip back to France is even more likely. No one else would even know who she is."

"True."

"I tested out the doors with Lulu. It was definitely the door to the stairwell that I heard last night."

"Which opens the door, so to speak, to the suspect being anyone on the ship, crew and passenger alike."

"I suppose it's more likely it was a crew member being the—oh, that's right, I almost forgot. Benny mentioned something about Gerard being taken away by security this morning, right in front of the rest of the staff!"

"Goodness, Penelope, you and your friends could put the entire NYPD to shame," Richard marveled.

She smiled, then frowned in thought. "Oh dear."

"What is it?"

"I think my plan to learn more might only create more waves." Pen sighed. "I'm afraid we are going to have to incorporate Kitty into this."

His mouth hitched up on one side. "I never thought I'd hear you say that."

"It's the lesser of two evils, sadly." She thought of the security officer who had gone perfectly ashen back in the office: Alain. "I see no reason to get someone into any more trouble than he's in. Besides, my way may get us more answers. The most important being, what happened to Marie Blanchet?"

CHAPTER NINETEEN

P<small>ENELOPE AND</small> R<small>ICHARD ARRIVED AT THE CAFÉ, WHERE</small> all her friends were still there. They were done with their lunch, and were chatting away. Pen had always assumed she was the glue holding them together, but they seemed to be awfully chummy in her absence. She was surprised to find their heads leaned together, conversing with a relish that meant it had to be about a particular murder.

"You all seemed to be getting along smashingly," Pen noted with a wry look as she joined them at the tables.

"We were discussing what you might have been up to... without us," Kitty said accusingly.

"Well, now I'm including you out of necessity."

"But first, you're getting something to eat," Richard reminded her as he pulled up a seat next to her.

"Here, this was your anchovy sandwich." Benny wrinkled his nose with distaste as he pushed it her way.

Pen devoured it, relishing the feel of something to stop the grumbling in her stomach. It was one of her favorite quick meals. Everyone waited with a mixture of amusement and impatience. When she was done, washing it down with a glass of lemonade, she sighed with satisfaction.

"Can you tell us now?" Kitty urged.

"Yes, yes," Pen said. She turned to Kitty. "I know the name of the security officer who told your source. I need you to contact her for a meeting."

Kitty's mouth set with a reluctance to answer.

"Oh for heaven's sake Kitty, you can trust Penelope," Cousin Cordelia said, her voice shrill with impatience.

"It's for the greater good, Kitty. I need him to give me more information and if I call and ask to speak with him directly, Alfred will know that he was the one to tell your source. In fact, if any of us call specifically for him, it would look suspicious. Alfred had to know I was trying to flush out one of his men. If it wasn't for the phone call that came, he would have tried to—"

Pen stopped realizing she had inadvertently said too much. Then, too late, she realized coming to an abrupt stop only made it more obvious.

"What about this phone call?" Lulu asked, reading her like a book.

Pen turned to Richard. He sighed. "I don't like revealing it this way, but I suppose they have a right to know. It will get around the ship soon enough and if it helps find the killer—or confirm that they have the right killer in custody—then it's all for the better."

With Richard's reassurance, Pen turned back to everyone else. The café wasn't quite as full, the lunch period of the day coming to an end. Thus, they had all the privacy they needed. She told them everything that had happened in the security office, from flushing out the blabbermouth security officer to the phone call about Marie's body being found.

Her friends were even more animated than the security team had been. Pen allowed them to air their questions and comments and exclamations. Cousin Cordelia needed a moment to fan herself before they continued. Once they were settled, Penelope told them her plan.

"So now that you have the name of the security officer, I need you to contact your source, Kitty. This has to go through her so it won't look suspicious. I told you Alain's name, now can you tell me yours?"

"No," Kitty said.

It wasn't just Penelope who protested with outrage. Kitty held her hand up to silence everyone before she continued.

"I *will*, however, introduce you, Penelope, and only you. I think that's fair for the greater good. There is no reason everyone else has to know who she is."

"But—"

Kitty held her hand up to silence her. "It isn't a matter of trust. I'm sure everyone here is perfectly trustworthy, with one possible exception." She took a moment to glare at Benny before she continued. "It's a matter of integrity. I have to maintain my journalistic morals for my source's sake. You and only you, Pen."

Pen remained silent, seething inside at Kitty's stubbornness. It bordered on deception, though she appreciated her sticking to her guns.

"She'll do it," Lulu finally said in her stead. When Pen gave her an exasperated look, she arched her brow. "We're trying to find a killer not run a gossip magazine. I'm fine not knowing if it means solving a murder. And I'm sure everyone here agrees with me," she hinted.

"Lucille is right," Richard agreed. "Do what you need to do, Penelope."

Benny and Cousin Cordelia both remained petulantly disappointed, which was no surprise, but eventually nodded.

Twenty minutes later, Penelope was with Kitty in her cabin waiting for Léa to appear. It was a First Class cabin, though not a suite. Still, it was as luxurious as any of the other First Class amenities.

Kitty had called for some innocent request to get the maid to come. In retrospect, Pen wasn't surprised it was that particular maid, yet again. Léa certainly had a flair for gossip. It seemed avarice was yet another of her vices. Pen wondered just how much Kitty had paid her.

At the knock on the door, both women sat up straighter. Kitty rushed to open it. Léa's smile faltered when she walked in and saw Penelope sitting with an expectant look on her face.

"I apologize in advance," Kitty began as she guided Léa to one of the chairs in the seating area of her cabin. "But for the sake of justice, I had to tell Penelope Banks here about you and what you told me earlier about the missing gun."

Léa was understandably irate, her green eyes sending shards of animosity Pen's way. She didn't spare Kitty either. She muttered incomprehensible French under her breath and instantly rose to leave.

"I know it was Alain who told you about the missing gun. I need information related to that gun. I could go directly through him, but if I go that route, it will alert Monsieur Duval, and Alain will get into trouble. How long before that trouble trickles down to you, Léa?"

That stopped her, and she turned to give a sour look to Penelope. "How do you mean?"

Pen told her what her plan was. After another bout of

French curses under her breath. She tried to plead her case. "He'll be angry with me!"

"He'll be even more angry with you if he knew there was a way to do this without getting him into trouble, and you refused. If a request to meet came from you, no one would think anything of it."

"Except that I am desperate for his attention. *I* do not call a man; *he* is the one always pestering me." She sniffed, her nose turned up at the very idea.

Penelope wanted to laugh at her stubborn audacity and misplaced priorities. Fortunately, Léa seemed to realign them on her own. She probably assumed that Pen or Kitty might tattle on her as well if she didn't help them. Pen would never be quite that underhanded, but she saw no reason to reveal that to Léa.

"Fine, I will do it," she spat, then gave Pen a cool look. "But he and I only meet in areas off-limits to passengers."

"You seem like an intelligent woman. I'm sure you can find a location convenient for all of us."

She scowled before giving a curt nod. "The Third Class level. Gerard is not so picky about us being there outside of work." Her nose wrinkled at the mention of his name.

Léa rose, giving Pen and Kitty an expectant look. "Are you coming, or not?"

"You can get him to come so quickly?" Kitty asked with skepticism.

By way of response, Léa returned a coy smile that threatened to become a sneer of disdain. *"Bien sûr."*

Penelope and Kitty looked at one another, then rose. Léa led them to the stairwell, the same that Pen was certain Vivian's murderer had escaped to. She paid close attention as they were led down to the Second Class, then Third Class levels. Léa had them exit there, but Pen noted that there was a door labeled Staff/Personnel beyond that level. She tried the door, and wasn't surprised to find it locked.

The corridors on the Third Class level were much narrower, almost to a claustrophobic degree. The doors were also much closer together, meaning there probably wasn't much room in each cabin. The Art Deco aesthetic was decidedly missing on this level, the walls bare and stark white with uncarpeted flooring. Pen and Kitty followed Léa to a large dining hall which was a plain room with long communal tables and chairs. It was well past lunchtime and too early for dinner, but the room was presumably more spacious than the sleeping quarters so she wasn't surprised to see so many people simply sitting at tables without eating or drinking anything.

Léa walked to a phone next to the door to the kitchen. She narrowed her eyes at her two companions as she asked to be connected to the security office.

"Allô, David?" Léa's eyes went wide, eyelashes batting to match the suddenly coquettish tone in her voice. Pen could imagine how easily it melted the man on the other end of the line. She continued in French. "*I need to see Alain, it is very important.*".... "*Oh? An important security matter? What is it?*" Eyes glittering with devilish interest. "*Yes, of course. But surely Monsieur Duval doesn't need all of you?*" ... "*Of course it is important, very important.*" Her eyes narrowed with impatient contempt. "*Yes, and it is best he come as soon as he can. I am in the Third Class dining room.*" The kittenish smile was back. "*You will? Thank you, my peanut.*"

Pen bit back a smile at the term of endearment, which must have had a certain meaning in French that didn't translate to her American ear.

Léa hung up the phone and all hints of her flirtatious

airs disappeared underneath the scowl she reserved for Pen and Kitty. "Now, we wait."

She brushed past the two of them to sit at the end of one of the tables. It was well away from anyone else in the dining room, where they could afford some bit of privacy. Pen and Kitty joined her. While they waited, Penelope decided to use the opportunity to learn more about Marie from a fellow maid. It was probably good that Léa didn't know Marie's body had only recently been found.

"Did you know Marie Blanchet, the maid who...went missing?"

Léa narrowed her eyes, as though wondering if there was a trap in that question. "Of course I did. I shared a room with her."

"Were you two close?"

Léa sniffed and shrugged. "Marie was polite, but I could see she thought she was not meant for life on a ship, especially as a maid. She wanted to be one of the waitresses in the bar." Léa laughed with derision. "That is the most prized position, of course. Nice, fat American tips. We all want it. We even pretend sometimes, just to practice. We steal the long black gloves and empty bottles of champagne and pretend to serve. But one has to know someone, or earn your way to that position, and of course be very pretty." She shot them a very pretty, pert smile. She then arched a brow rich with meaning as she bored into them with her gaze. "Of course, being a maid gives you other benefits...."

"You'll earn your nice, fat American tip for this," Pen said in a wry tone.

Léa pursed her lips with satisfaction before continuing. "Marie felt cleaning was beneath her. She was lucky she spoke English well enough to work in First Class. I was the one to point out that if she were lucky, she could find a nice, wealthy patron. She seemed insulted even by that!" Léa gave them a look of bewilderment, as though there was nothing unsavory about her suggestion. "She eventually learned though, found her patron. She was a bit smug about it."

"How so?"

"Well, she would not stop talking about shopping in New York, quitting and moving to Paris from Calais when she returned. I told her she shouldn't be so boastful, particularly in front of Gerard. At that, she scoffed, as though even he could not touch her."

Pen and Kitty exchanged a look.

"So you think it was a wealthy patron who murdered her?"

"It had to be. She got too greedy I assume, no?" Léa studied them more intently.

"Could it have been blackmail?"

Léa's eyes went wide in thought. "That does make more sense. Marie was not fit to play *le chaton*. Too much like—how do you say it, like...sandpaper?"

"Abrasive."

"*Oui*. Poor Hugo wasted his effort on her, she is not meant for love with a simple barman. But she was very cunning—quiet. She could get anyone to talk. Those big blue eyes, staring like a little duckling, waiting for croutons of information to come tumbling out." She frowned as though those big blue eyes had worked on her as well. Pen wondered what it was Léa had revealed. She debated being tactless enough to ask, but they were interrupted by a new arrival.

"*What is it, Léa!*" An irritated Alain, came bursting through the entrance to the dining room, a look of consternation on his face as French spilled from his lips. *"There is a serious matter that—"*

Alain stopped when he recognized Penelope sitting at the table with Léa. He shot an angry glance toward the latter. "What is this?"

"They know it was you who told me," Léa said, shooting an accusatory look right back to him.

"I—" He looked at Penelope, and realized how his secret had been discovered. He stood straighter and gave her a steady look. He wisely walked over to sit with them, out of hearing distance of the Third Class passengers, who had certainly taken an interest in what was happening. "What is it you want from me, Mademoiselle Banks?"

Penelope got straight to the point. "I want to know if Gerard was the one who stole the gun."

Léa gasped, no longer irritated at having been embroiled in this mess. She looked at Alain with avid curiosity coloring her eyes.

"What? No!" He looked even more alarmed and white-faced than he had when Pen had sussed him out earlier. "Where did you hear such a thing?" He shot Léa a hard look.

"It was not me!"

"Why did security take him away this morning?" Pen asked, not interested in watching the two of them get into a fight.

Alain swallowed hard, not answering.

"Alain—may I call you that?" Pen continued, more gently now.

He gave her a confused look and nodded.

"Alain, I am trying to save an innocent man from being accused of murder. Or, if you prefer, prove Raul was indeed the one to kill Vivian. I have no intention of revealing that you were the one to tell me anything. Why do you think I had Léa call you instead of doing so myself—that would have instantly made you suspect."

A flash of gratitude colored his eyes, but they remained wary. "It was not Gerard who stole the gun. We are certain of it, well, almost certain."

"So why was he taken?"

He paused, a hand coming to his forehead and pressing as though he could squeeze out the right way to proceed. Pen decided to help him along.

"Did it have *anything* to do with Vivian's murder? Is it even tangentially related?"

"Non, no!" He finally said, dropping his hand and facing Pen again. "It was a misunderstanding."

"Well there should be no harm in you telling us, then," Kitty urged.

He narrowed his eyes at her. "You are the reporter for the newspaper, no?"

"She is," Léa answered, her eyes slits as she stared at Kitty.

Alain became agitated. "I cannot—"

"She won't report on this," Pen said, giving Kitty a pressing look.

Kitty remained stubborn. "I can promise I will keep my sources anonymous."

Alain looked incredulous.

"There's no way to trace any information back to either of you. Right now, David in the security office believes your only sin is a tryst with a fellow crew member. Perhaps a bit negligent, considering what is currently happening, but hardly worthy of anything more than a slight scolding."

"Unless Léa decides to tell someone else. She is not trustworthy." He gave her an accusing look again.

"Do you think I want to get in trouble as well?"

"Both of you, please," Pen said, before they began to fight. "I just need to know why he was taken is all."

Alain exhaled with anger, then answered. "Yesterday, he made a call into the security office, the lower office, with an urgent matter. He needed both men. It was...against protocol, but both men left—I won't give you their names!"

"That's fine," Pen said, in a voice encouraging him to continue.

"They did lock the door, and as there was no prisoner at the time, it seemed safe enough to leave the office empty for a moment to address the matter. When they arrived there was nothing, no one there. Gerard insisted it wasn't he who had called. The bartenders can attest to the fact that he was berating them for the sloppy positioning of the bottles behind the bar at the time."

"So it was a ploy by someone pretending to be Gerard to pull the men away from the office," Pen confirmed. "And that was when the gun was taken."

Alain nodded. "We only discovered after Mademoiselle Adler was murdered."

Pen turned to Léa. "I won't keep you from your duties any longer."

Léa wasn't stupid. Penelope hadn't said anything to Alain about leaving, which meant they were going to discuss something that could prove to be fodder for gossip.

"No." She crossed her arms and remained seated.

"I should go as well," Alain said, frowning at her.

Pen sighed, realizing she wasn't winning this battle and spat out before he could stand up, "Tell me more about finding Marie Blanchet's body."

CHAPTER TWENTY

ALAIN STOPPED IN HIS TRACKS. HE SLOWLY TURNED around to face Penelope. "So you understood the phone call earlier in the security office."

Penelope stared back, not answering, not that he had asked it as a question. She wanted him to tell her about Marie Blanchet's body, and he would either indulge her or he wouldn't.

"I cannot speak on that!" Alain insisted.

"I assume she was found on the ship, but at least tell me if she died within the past twenty-four hours?" It was really a two-part question, and Pen was hoping he'd at least give her one of the answers.

"It was...recent," he conceded. "She was found in the storage area for the deck chairs on the upper deck. She was out of sight of the passengers, *Dieu merci!*"

Léa inhaled sharply, but she appeared to be more intrigued than distraught.

"This remains here, Léa," Penelope warned.

"Of course," she said, showing far too much innocence in her expression to be believed.

"It does not matter," Alain said with a sigh, as he took a seat again. "News like this will spread. I told him we should have made an announcement about Vivian, but he wanted to conduct his investigation, make sure we had the right man. Unlike last time, when Marie disappeared only the night before docking, we cannot contain this."

"So none of us were able to enjoy New York," Léa said petulantly. "All for no reason. Where has she been?"

"That is what we are trying to find out," Alain said, looking perfectly perplexed.

"So she has been hiding on board this entire time?" Kitty asked.

"Apparently so. We are questioning the staff to see if anyone helped her."

All three turned to Léa.

"It was not me!"

That wasn't too difficult to believe. Léa seemed like the type to look out mostly for herself. Besides, Penelope was far more concerned with Marie's murder than who had been hiding her.

Another thing that nagged at her: why remain hidden on board when Marie could reveal herself and whoever she had been hiding from at any point? Was it because they were too powerful? Too dangerous? Was it because she had done something wrong, perhaps even illegal, and didn't want to face the consequences? But if it was blackmail, surely the victim had just as much reason to pretend nothing happened and stay silent.

Except, they obviously hadn't.

The real question was how did they manage to flush out Marie and then kill her? The timing with Vivian's murder was just too coincidental. They had to be connected....

"Was Marie blonde?"

Everyone turned to her in confusion.

"She was," Léa, quickly answered. "*Pourquoi?*"

Pen ignored her to interrogate Alain. "Was she wearing a tuxedo when you found her, like the ones the male staff were wearing during the departure party?"

His brow rose in alarm. "Only the white shirt and black pants, but...how do you know this!"

"And the long black gloves?" The ones that were so easy to steal to practice being a waitress. "Was she wearing those too, or were they at least—"

All three women flinched in surprise as Alain shot up from his seat and stared at Penelope in horror. "*Mon Dieu!*"

"What is it?" Kitty asked. "What did she say that's got you buzzing?"

Alain collected himself and his eyes hardened. "Mademoiselle Banks, I insist that you come with me."

"What? Where?"

"Please stand. I will take you by force if I have to."

"Surely you don't suspect me?" Pen almost laughed in surprise.

"Please, Mademoiselle Banks, do not make this more difficult than necessary," he said.

"This is absurd!"

She yelped in surprise as he took hold of her arm and forced her out of her seat.

"Wait a moment..." she protested, trying to reason with him even as he practically dragged her away.

Pen stopped resisting, realizing this was going to happen, no matter what. In fact, perhaps it was a good thing. She had obviously said something important, enough to draw suspicion to herself, at least as far as a clue to Marie's murder went.

Whereas, Penelope had just figured out that Marie was likely the one to kill Vivian.

She twisted around to face Kitty. "Tell Richard, I've been taken to the security office below deck," she said, assuming that was where Alain was taking her. She no longer resisted and he held her with a loosened grip as he took her away. In the stairwell, they descended a floor and he used a key to take her past the staff door to the lower levels banned to passengers.

Penelope played the possible scenario in her head, and it began to make sense. Marie's belongings had probably been taken to a secure area once her disappearance was noted. That left her only the option of staff clothing to change into, no doubt brought by the person hiding her. Pen had to assume it was a male staff member, if she was wearing the tuxedo, or parts of it when she was found. That certainly didn't limit the suspects.

Still, that tuxedo had made it rather convenient when Marie decided to murder the person she was hiding from. No one would bat an eye at someone in a tuxedo, especially on the First Class level. The top hat would also mask the fact that she was a woman, so long as she wore it low enough on her head. And the towels—well, that was one thing Pen couldn't really explain. In retrospect, Richard had been right, the gun could have much more easily been hidden underneath a coat. So why bring towels?

That, and why Marie had wanted to kill Vivian.

It had to be blackmail. Suddenly, Vivian's interest in investigating her fellow passengers made more sense. What better way to divert attention from herself, especially in front of a New York detective and private investigator? She must have been terrified when she heard that, wondering if it was something more than a coincidence. No wonder she had discussed it with Raul.

Of course, Marie must have been just as terrified, learning that the person she'd been hiding from was once again on the ship. She'd obviously decided to put an end to it. Permanently.

So, what information did Marie have on Vivian that was worthy of blackmail?

More importantly, if Marie had killed Vivian, who had killed Marie?

They reached the security office, which was now abuzz with activity. It came to a sudden, and quite irritated stop when Alain marched in with Penelope.

"I have Mademoiselle Banks, who should be considered a suspect in the murder of Marie Blanchet."

"Now, wait just one moment, I didn't kill Marie!"

Alfred scrutinized the two of them, then addressed Alain. "Why do you suspect her?"

"She knows everything about her murder, specifically what she was wearing. She even knew about the gloves!"

"I can explain that."

"She even knew Marie's hair color, without having met her, *supposedly*."

"That was a guess, based on prior information that has yet to be imparted to you. My cousin, Mrs. Cordelia Davies, she saw Marie earlier on our floor, trying to get into Vivian's suite."

"And you refrained from telling us this information, why?"

"I didn't have a chance to." Not necessarily true, but Pen saw no reason to be such a stickler for the truth.

"A likely story," Alain scoffed.

"But it all ultimately paints Marie as Vivian's killer, don't you see?"

That had everyone frowning in surprise.

"Explain," Alfred said, no doubt hoping she would continue to dig her own grave.

Penelope did, if only to help them see the truth, at least what she thought was the truth. "During the maiden voyage, Marie, who was apparently known to be good at getting people to talk—" She turned to Alain for confirmation, but he wisely gave nothing away. "—must have discovered something about Vivian, something worth blackmailing her over. Her fellow staff can attest to the fact that she had been boasting about some pile of kale she was about to get, quitting and moving to Paris. I can assume the pay here isn't enough to do that after one trip?"

No one confirmed, but one member of security did snort with disdain. He received a harsh look from Alfred, who then turned back to Penelope. "Continue."

"It obviously didn't go as planned. I'm not sure what happened, but Marie must have felt it was safer to hide. Then, when she learned Vivian was on the boat returning to France, either she wanted revenge or felt her life was in danger so she murdered her instead. In fact, I'd bet Marie was the one who stole the gun. Surely you can see that?"

"I see nothing but conjecture, Mademoiselle Banks."

Penelope sighed. "The gloves found with her body—"

Once again, everyone in the room stiffened in surprise, just as Alain had.

"What is it about them that is so damning?"

"You seem to know so much about this case, perhaps you can tell me."

Everyone in the room stared at Penelope with a piercing intensity that was overwhelming. "I...I was just going to point out that you can probably still smell the gunpowder on them. I smelled it, very faintly, in the hallway through which she escaped. That would confirm that she fired the gun."

Alfred studied her, conflict flickering in his gaze.

"Is there another importance they have?"

A few of the men eyed each other, which meant that there was.

"Wait...how was she killed?"

"That is privileged information, Mademoiselle—"

"She was strangled, wasn't she? With one of the gloves!"

"And just how do you—?"

"Oh stop, it doesn't take a private investigator to figure out as much. That's why Alain took custody of me as soon as I mentioned them. If you'll speak with my cousin, she'll tell you exactly what she saw, someone at Vivian's door wearing those gloves! That and carrying a set of clean towels."

"Towels?" Alfred wore an expression of puzzlement.

"Marie was holding towels when she first tried to enter Vivian's suite. That was when my cousin saw her, and she quickly ran away. She must have later returned to finish what she started."

"This story is getting more and more absurd," Alain said. "I participated in the search of the suite. There was only one extra set of towels, which we know Elise had brought up earlier."

"So perhaps she didn't bring towels the second time she successfully entered the suite. But you have the gloves. I'm sure if you investigate it, you'll learn more...about *both* murders." Pen gave Alfred a meaningful look.

"All the same, we have no reason to release Monsieur García. At least until we speak with Madame Davies and learn more about this person she saw. For the safety of the passengers and crew, we must keep him in custody for now."

"This is an outrage!"

"It is our policy, but rest assured, you have given us new information with which to conduct our investigation. We will be interviewing your cousin to confirm what she saw, now that it has been conveniently related to us." He gave Pen an admonishing look. "*Alors*, Alain, if you will escort Mademoiselle Banks back to the passenger areas?"

Penelope didn't bother arguing. She cast one last quick gaze to the holding cell where Raul was, then preceded Alain out of the office. Alfred Duval's stubbornness was all the motivation she needed to continue investigating. And she knew exactly where to go next.

CHAPTER TWENTY-ONE

Alain planted Penelope right outside the door to the staff area after escorting her from the security office.

"Please stay out of this investigation, Mademoiselle Banks," he warned. His expression softened before adding, "*Merci* for not telling Monsieur Duval about my...transgression."

With that, he promptly closed the door and left her to her own devices. She assumed, after so long, that the others wouldn't still be waiting in the café for her, so she decided to return to her suite. She wanted to quickly freshen up before continuing with her investigation. When Penelope arrived on her floor, only Kitty and Richard were waiting by her door.

"I told the others to relax and enjoy themselves, that you'd be back by dinner and answer all their questions then," Richard said, explaining why the others weren't there. She was sure he had framed it as more of an order than a suggestion, and for that she was grateful.

"That's probably for the best. I need to interview someone. We should probably go soon, before—"

"Now, wait just a moment, Penelope. You've nearly been taken into custody once already. And it seems we have a second unknown murderer on our hands. Don't tell me you're intent on continuing with this investigation?"

"All the more so now. They refused to release Raul, even after I explained how it was obviously Marie who killed Vivian."

"What?"

Pen turned to Kitty. "You didn't tell him anything?"

"You insisted on discretion."

"Of all the times to be discrete," Pen said with a sigh. She quickly told Richard everything that she had learned, up to and including Marie being strangled with the black glove.

"Marie's death doesn't completely absolve Raul of Vivian's death. You don't have very much to tie her to that murder. Honestly, even your cousin's observation of a stranger at Vivian's door can't directly be tied to Vivian's death. For all we know, it could have been a member of the staff trying to bring more towels."

"Unless they find there is gunpowder on the black gloves she wore. The smell should still linger."

He tilted his head to the side in acknowledgment. "That is a good point. But who's to say *she* was wearing them at the time? Perhaps the person who killed her was the one wearing them."

Pen hadn't considered that. It brought things back to square one.

"Perhaps we should focus on the towels instead. I'm thinking you were right, there must be more to them than just hiding a gun. I think the towels were just a distraction or prop or—"

Both Richard and Kitty stared, long enough for the latter to get impatient when Pen didn't explain her sudden pause.

"Well? What is it?"

"Prop—*pop*! *That's* why she had the towels. It was to mask the sound of the gunshot. Richard, you know how loud a gun is, especially in such tight quarters. Perhaps Marie knew as well and came prepared. But even that couldn't fully mask the sound. When I first heard it, I thought someone in the hallway had been popping champagne or some balloons from the party. Raul said nothing about the towels being near her body or the gun. Marie must have taken them with her."

"Okay, then those towels should be somewhere on the ship," Richard said.

"Simone will confirm Raul didn't have them when he left...just in case certain people think I'm too biased in his favor." Pen arched a brow and Richard met it with one of his own.

"That still leaves motive," Kitty said with a meaningful clearing of her throat. "*Why* would Marie kill Vivian?"

"She disappeared for a reason. If we can discover that reason, that may cinch the case against her and Raul will be cleared."

"Did Vivian's ghost kill Marie? Because we appear to have the old chicken and egg conundrum on our hands. Who killed who first?" Kitty asked.

"Perhaps Vivian wasn't the only person Marie had been blackmailing. She may have figured out the so-called siblings' secret early on, especially if she was the one assigned to their room. Then there is Edwin and whatever his father is so skittish about."

"All things for the security team to figure out. Once those towels are found, hopefully with evidence of them being used to suppress a gunshot, then we've cleared Raul, and your duty is done," Richard said.

"Oh, that reminds me, we have to go to the bar!"

"What?"

Rather than answer, she grabbed his hand and rushed him toward the stairs. Kitty quickly followed them.

"Penelope!"

"I'll explain when we get there!"

Blessedly, Richard allowed himself to be dragged along. He probably knew there was no point in arguing when Penelope was on a mission. He couldn't deny that her hunches often panned out, and he was just a bit curious himself.

It was well into the afternoon, which many a First Class passenger took as a sign it was time for drinks. To Penelope's dismay, there were only two men behind the bar, neither of which was Hugo. She approached all the same and got the attention of the closest one whose badge read: Marc.

He was sliding two tumblers filled with amber liquid to one of the women in a black dress, heeled shoes, and long gloves.

"Is Hugo here?"

Marc squinted one eye at her. "He's quite the popular man today. No, he was—he is elsewhere," he quickly corrected. Like most of the staff, he had a slight French accent.

She leaned in to speak in a more confidential tone. "Was he taken by security?"

The surprise on his face was palpable, then he narrowed his eyes. "I shouldn't say."

"That's okay, you don't have to." She paused before

continuing, taking on a more somber expression. "Was he terribly broken up about Marie's disappearance?"

Marc shot her a wary look, and twisted his mouth to one side before softly chuckling. "I told him that would lead nowhere. She was not interested in anyone on this ship, not the crew, at any rate. I can always tell when a woman likes to use men only for what they offer."

"Did she use poor Hugo?" Pen asked with a dose of sympathy.

"Only to try and work here as one of the girls." He jerked his chin toward the waitresses. "That was not going to happen."

"Hmm," Pen said nodding. Léa had already said as much.

Before he could speak again, a pretty waitress arrived with an order for him. While he made the drinks, Pen eyed the bottles behind the bar, remembering that Alain had said Gerard had been in the bar dictating the arrangement of the bottles when a phone call had come to the security office, supposedly from him. To his credit, everything did look neat and pristine. In fact, everything on board would pass the white glove test.

"You were one of the waiters who brought out champagne during the departure party." It was a statement, not a question. Pen had every face right there in her head like a photograph. "The white gloves you used, are they kept with all the other uniforms?"

He shook his head, rolling his eyes. "Those are delivered right back to the launders after each use. Monsieur Gerard is very strict on that. We get perfectly clean, white ones directly from them as well, those that use them in their job."

That explained the black gloves.

By the time Marc was done with the drinks, she had an inkling of another clue. "How rigorously does the ship get cleaned in between arrival and departure?"

He coughed out a laugh. "Canard is a tyrant about that, even worse than when the passengers are on board."

"Including the brass door handles, I presume?"

"Oh yes. 'Everything must sparkle, shine, and glow!'" Marc mimicked, then looked slightly abashed.

"Are all the bartenders so good at impressions of Gerard?" she asked with a girlish laugh, as though she were simply flirting. Richard, standing next to her didn't so much as twitch, to his credit.

"Hugo is the best, he's the one I learned from. 'That nasally voice and flowery touch with only the barest hint of that *commandant* residue'," he said with a slight sneer, which he quickly erased, remembering he had an audience.

Pen wondered who else Hugo had taught to impersonate Gerard. Marc's was passable, certainly enough to convince someone over the phone.

"Commandant? He was a major?" Richard asked in surprise.

Marc gave him a look tinged with irony as he nodded, and a mild, humorless smile came to his face. Something passed unspoken between them before he continued. "The war was good for some, no?"

Now, Penelope understood that look. They were both veterans of the Great War. Poor Marc must have been a baby, just barely old enough to be commandeered into service. Pen knew enough about the military, the American military, at any rate—she'd once flipped through a book that had plainly displayed the rankings—to know that a major was high enough to be distanced from the frontlines if one wanted it that way. It couldn't have been seniority alone that had Gerard ranking so highly, which meant that he must have followed the path of nepotism.

"From Commandant Canard to Monsieur Canard, Director of Hospitality on an ocean liner," she remarked. "Usually military men stay that way until retirement, even with no war to fight."

Marc's brow quirked, as though there was definitely a story there, one which was a poorly kept secret.

"What do you know?" Pen asked, taking on the role of a dimwitted, flighty thing, whose only interest in life was idle gossip.

Marc shot her a wry look, teasingly admonishing her for being so nosy.

"Oh, come now. I promise not to tell. Besides, you must have found out from someone else?"

He seemed to be mulling it over, and eventually spoke. "Not while in the war, mind you—he behaved himself then. But after that, he...propositioned the wrong person. That uncle or cousin or whoever protected him from the German border was not so forgiving about such things. Best to send him away for a while."

"I see," Pen said in wonder. Mentally, she was connecting the man she knew with the worst-case scenario in terms of "propositioning," and it made sense. Paris may have been liberated about such things, but the Old Guard was always far more conservative. And Gerard was not so young.

"I assume it's spread among all the staff by now?"

"I only heard it from Hugo."

"Not Léa?" Pen asked, ignoring the irate look Kitty gave her.

Marc snorted. "That's another one who likes to use men. If it wasn't for Elise, I would think all the First Class maids were snakes." There was a fleeting look of soft tenderness in his eyes at the mention of the only virtuous maid. He gave Pen a quick rueful look. "Though of course what happened to Marie is a shame."

Pen wasn't going to be the one to tell him the truth about what really happened to Marie. It would raise too many questions from him, and right now she only wanted answers.

Unfortunately, two waitresses arrived for new orders, cutting short her brief interrogation. He shot Penelope an apologetic look, then moved further down the bar to accommodate them.

Penelope turned around to lean against the bar and face Richard and Kitty.

"Hugo is the key. I think he was taken away because they suspect he was the one hiding Marie. I wish I could have spoken to him before that."

"Rest assured, they are probably asking the same questions you would have, Penelope," Richard said. "There isn't some agenda to lay the blame on Raul if he isn't the murderer."

"Are you sure about that?"

"At the very least, they'd be a bit more direct. I don't know why you have to be so circumspect in your interrogations, Pen," Kitty protested. "I would have had all the same answers in half the time."

"There is something to be said for delicacy, Kitty. If I left things up to you—"

Once again, she stopped short, her eyes having landed on another fruitful source of information. Both Kitty and Richard followed her gaze to see Edwin in a corner, drowning his sorrows in something much stronger than any neophyte to the drinking world such as himself could handle.

"Speaking of a delicate touch, I'd like to handle this boy-o on my own, if you don't mind."

CHAPTER TWENTY-TWO

Edwin looked even worse the closer Penelope got to him in the Clair de Lune Bar. His face was actually streaked with tears as he stared down into his drink. He may have been new to drinking, but he looked far too reminiscent of men she'd seen who never seemed to claw their way back out of their cups.

Penelope was close enough to practically bump right into his table before he even noticed her, or at least before his eyes focused enough to take him away from whatever dark thoughts he was harboring.

"I can only imagine how devastating this has been for you," she said in a sympathetic voice as she gingerly took the seat across from him.

Edwin viciously wiped at his eyes with the back of his hands, trying to erase any evidence of what most men (very likely his own father) viewed as weakness. He sniffed up the rest and sat up straighter.

"I...I just, I'm not quite sure how to proceed."

"Vivian meant that much to you?"

His eyelashes, so pale they were nearly invisible, fluttered for a brief moment before extending to their limits to reveal wide, guileless blue eyes.

"I apologize, Mrs....?"

"*Mademoiselle* Banks, but please, call me Penelope. And you're Edwin?"

"I am. Edwin Pembrook."

"Did you at least manage to get that last drink with Vivian?" Pen asked with a sympathetic smile.

A brief, tragic smile appeared on his lips, but disappeared just as quickly. A look of wonder came to his face. "She is—*was*...quite lovely."

Now, it was Pen's eyelashes that took a turn at fluttering, lost in the naked honesty of youth. Edwin seemed like a child, discovering the world for the first time.

The bitterness that came to erase every last trace of it was like a blast of cold air, bringing both of them back down to the reality of the murder that had occurred.

"Not quite what you expected for your eighteenth birthday, I take it?" Pen said, hoping the expression she sported leaned in a maternal direction, enough to ease him into revealing more about himself.

That was apparently the wrong thing to say. Edwin's mouth carried a sour note and he quickly finished off the rest of his drink, an alarmingly thick finger of liquid. He swung his head around, frowning until his eyes alit on a passing waitress.

"You there, one more whiskey, if you please!"

The waitress flashed a smile so forced it was worrisome. Pen was the one to ask him if he was certain he wanted another. Edwin drunkenly slashed a hand through the air, dismissing her concerns with an equally zozzled, "Bugger it all!"

Penelope and the waitress, "Antoinette" from her badge, made eye contact and shrugged.

If he was going to drown his sorrows, Pen figured she might as well grasp what she could from him before he went completely under. Perhaps Kitty had a point about being direct.

"What is it your father is so worried about? What is it he is shielding you from?"

He snorted derisively and glared at Penelope. "Everything."

"Why?" Pen pressed, hoping Antoinette was taking her time ordering that drink.

Edwin's eyes glazed over, and it appeared he was looking right through her at something else. She was certain she had already lost him before he finally spoke up.

"It wasn't supposed to be me, you know. I was, as they say, an afterthought. Everything should have gone to George. If not for that bloody war."

Penelope's eyes softened with understanding. "Was George your older brother?"

He exhaled long and slow, barely nodding in a somber manner.

"And he died in the Great War?"

This time the nod was even weaker.

"Is your father worried you might...die as well?"

He blubbered out a laugh, increasing in intensity until it was nearly maniacal. The waitress returned with his drink, looking even more concerned. Pen reached out to relieve her of it and she skittered away.

Edwin simmered down into a smoldering brood. "I do believe that is my drink you are holding, *Mademoiselle* Banks."

Pen held onto it. "Why don't you tell me more, Edwin. It's obviously a burden for you. Lay it on my shoulders."

His eyes seemed to contract, the blue irises hardening and brightening until he appeared perfectly sober. She thought for sure he would begin sobbing, but he caught himself.

"No one has ever asked me how I felt." Again, he had that awestruck look on his face.

"I am now," she urged.

He averted his gaze, and again she thought she had lost him until he spoke, erupting like a cracked dam.

"George came first. George Pembrook...*fils*."

"He's named after your father?" Pen never understood how men could be so prideful. Women never felt the need to name their daughters after themselves. Edwin really must have felt like an afterthought.

Edwin nodded. "The proud father with his perfect boy. The twelfth Earl of Greymoor. My brother would have been lucky number thirteen."

"An earl?"

A sardonic smile came to his face. "I was simply the insurance to keep that title in the family line. George was the oldest and only male heir. Three girls and they nearly gave up. Then I happened along. By then, the old man had placed all his chips decidedly on George's square. How is that for luck?"

"Were you close to your brother?"

He looked off to the side with a sentimental smile. "You would have thought being a future earl would make him pompous like so many entitled *lords of the manor* were, but no. He saw how neglected I was—even mother only concerned herself with the girls' *grand entrance into society*." There was a flourish in his voice that drenched the universal rite of passage for many a wealthy young woman in a coating of disdain. His smile brightened, as majestic as the clouds parting for the sun. "He was ten years older than me, but that didn't make a difference. Whether it was some insect or creature I'd discovered or some word I wanted to know the meaning of, he dropped everything to listen or answer. He had the same curious mind and love of nature. He taught me all about bird watching, could navigate his way around the dense woods near us as though by magic, and loved showing me secret places he'd found. Wouldn't suffer anyone criticizing my ignorance or immaturity. Not even father."

A vicious smile curled his lips and something jagged reached his eyes. It was washed away by a sea of sorrow. "Then that bloody war came along. We all held our breath hoping it would be resolved by the time he was old enough to be dragged into it, but no. Father could have pulled strings to settle him into a more favorable situation, but George wouldn't hear of it. Not when the sons of our own staff and the local villagers were going to the front.

"And for a while, he survived. Made it into some secret wing of the military he couldn't talk about." His brow furrowed with something Pen couldn't quite place, confusion or dismay. "When he died, the reports weren't clear— some rubbish about national security. Even at eight years old I could tell when someone was pulling one over. Father was never successful about getting a straight answer, which meant someone even higher than him had screwed the pooch, as they say.

"And then there was *moi*. No more lolling about—standards to uphold, shoes to fill, and such." He sighed and looked off. "Which meant no ill-considered matches, at least not serious ones. And I was nothing but serious for Angela."

If the dear boy had seemed smitten with Vivian, he was positively spellbound by whoever this Angela was if the faraway look in his eyes was any indication.

"But she was the daughter of...*le petit bourgeois*," he snorted at the French insertion, "a shopkeep and his wife. And that just wouldn't do. So away to France we went! A bit of art and culture in Paris. Then, he suggested a trip to New York, a chance to experience the world, but again, only with the right families. I'm sure he was hoping a wealthy American heiress might soothe my broken heart."

Hence the stay in Long Island, which was overflowing with young, wealthy heiresses, especially after Memorial Day.

"Did he pay Angela off?"

A knowing smile graced his lips. "Her family is now quite well-heeled, as they say. I received the telegram announcing her engagement while we were in New York. Father was so certain of it, he already had the return tickets booked." Edwin stared off, perfectly gobsmacked. Pen could suddenly imagine the small child that had pestered his older brother with some perplexing bit of adult nonsense that needed explaining.

A wisened look came to his eyes. "Well I learned, didn't I? I've become quite worldly, I'll have you know. A bright young thing, ripened and leavened by the scalding sun of reality."

"Still, some realities will always have an effect on you."

His brow wrinkled in confusion.

"Vivian's death?" She nodded toward the drink she'd set on the table between them.

He stared at it as though wondering how it got there. Then, he snatched it up and took a long swig. "Yes...Vivian. It shouldn't have surprised me as much as it did. After all,

I've already known death and loss. Now, I suppose even murder is no longer a mystery to me," he said in a tragically grief-stricken voice. He swallowed hard and gave Pen a look that was almost cunning. "I don't need George to explain things to me anymore. I've experienced it all. Now, as much as even he did."

Penelope wondered what was worse, the horrors of war, where death was not only common but expected, or the shocking murder of someone you knew, even if only in passing.

"The maid who cleaned your cabin on the original trip to America, was her name Marie?"

His gaze found focus as he tried to recall. "Yes, I believe so? Why?"

"Did Vivian discuss her with you at all during that drink you shared?"

He stared at her in confusion. "How did you know?"

It *was* a rather odd question, seeing as how most passengers were unaware of Marie's connection to Vivian.

"What did you discuss about Marie?"

He shrugged and took a sip, thinking it over. "She wanted to know if I ever spoke with her on a personal level, if I had gotten close to her at all. As though father would have allowed that." He snorted, then frowned again. "Why?"

Pen thought it wise to hold off telling him about yet another murder. She couldn't think of a reason why he may have killed Marie...or Vivian, if it turned out Marie had been killed first. Penelope still thought it more likely that Marie had killed Vivian. Either way, there was no big secret here, just an overprotective father ensuring a proper future for his remaining son.

"Here's a bit of wisdom from someone who would be

closer to your brother's age than yours, make this your last drink today."

A wry bit of humor touched his expression and he lifted his glass in salute as she stood up to leave.

"Well?" Kitty pressed, practically bouncing on the balls of her feet.

"He's a sorry Sam, that's for sure. A lot of hard lessons early on in life, but he's no cold-blooded killer."

"Anyone can be a killer," Kitty said, rolling her eyes at Penelope's appalling naïvety.

Pen took a sip of Richard's whiskey. "I shall keep that in mind, Kitty."

CHAPTER TWENTY-THREE

AFTER REVEALING EVERYTHING THAT EDWIN HAD TOLD her, Penelope decided to wander the ship, hoping to stumble upon one of the other potential suspects in Marie's murder. Richard had detached himself, seemingly to discuss the theory of the noise-suppressing towels with the security office.

That left Kitty attached to her hip.

"It has to be those Swedes," she said, hooking her arm through Pen's as though they were bosom friends.

"They're Norwegian, Kitty," Pen sighed, feeling suddenly weary. That talk with Edwin had left her drained of energy.

"Yes, Norwegian. That's even more suspicious."

"How so?" Pen wrinkled her brow in wonder at the sometimes inane utterances of her present company.

"Who really knows anything about Norwegians? The perfect cover. They could be anyone!"

"What in heaven's name does that mean?"

"You and I know at least a few Swedes. The Lindgren sisters, they were Swedish, and I think the Carlssons as well. I met a Danish boy in Detroit once, Erik Hansen. And one of the boys who delivers the mail at the *Register*, his father is from Finland, as it turns out. Do you know any Norwegians?"

"I don't personally know any Siamese either, but that doesn't make any who cross my path murder suspects."

"Unless a murder has occurred."

"I think perhaps I need a rest before dinner."

"Yes, we should wait to bring in the others to help solve this. That Lulu is surprisingly astute."

"Not so surprising if you spent as much time with her as I have."

"And Cousin Cordelia, her innocence can bring a refreshing perspective. Even Benny...well, he's Benny."

"Yes, and on that note, I think I will take a small respite before dinner." Pen carefully disentangled her arm from Kitty's. "I will see you then."

Pen had fallen fast asleep when she returned to her room. Such that she woke up later than expected. Underneath her door, she found an envelope. She quickly opened it and saw that security had finally decided to officially alert the passengers about both murders with a public announcement.

Printed on crisp white paper, there was the expected language about security working tirelessly to solve the crimes, that passengers need not worry as the murders were most likely related and both crimes of passion, and they had already narrowed down the suspects, who likely posed no danger to anyone else. It ended with an announcement for a special service in the ship's chapel for those who needed comfort or wanted to honor the deceased.

Penelope doubted that would do much to reassure the passengers. It would do absolutely nothing to quiet the scuttlebutt. It was interesting to note that they didn't mention they already had someone in custody. Did that mean they had released Raul?

Penelope was already late for dinner. After quickly washing up and changing into dinner attire, she rushed to open her door, only to find Richard standing there waiting for her.

"You waited for me?"

"I waited for you. Though, five more minutes and I would have been knocking on the door just to make sure you were alive. You have a bad habit of skipping meals when murder is on your mind, my dear."

Pen smiled, happy they were over their tiff. She took his offered arm and allowed him to escort her to dinner.

"Did you learn anything about the towels?"

"Security was understandably close-lipped, but I'm certain I put the idea in their head to look for them."

"I suppose you didn't learn anything about Hugo either."

"No, but they did seem to be working hard to investigate both murders. I suspect Raul will be released soon."

She heard the note of resentment when he uttered the name. "I hope you aren't judging me based on my unfortunate history with men." She tried to sound teasing, but Richard's grim look didn't soften.

"This business about Clifford wanting the painting, what could that be about?"

"I honestly don't know." Now, she was the one with a hint of resentment in her voice. "I only told him I'd spent time with a boy named Raul back in Spain. I certainly didn't mention anything about posing for a painting. I suppose this is providence at work, intervening so I get the painting that should have gone to me in the first place. I must say, Madame Providence does have a rather morbid sense of humor."

"Yes. I for one am curious to see this painting."

Penelope swallowed, wondering what he would think of it when he finally did.

They reached the dining room where everyone else was already seated at their table.

"We weren't sure if you were having the chicken or the roast beef so we left it to you to decide if you wanted a glass of white or red wine," Cousin Cordelia said.

At least they didn't instantly assault her with questions. Hopefully, Kitty had already related the latest information. She caught Richard's eye as she sat across from him. He smiled and winked, which made her blood run a bit warmer.

Pen quickly decided the roast beef was the perfect thing to fill a stomach that had only had an anchovy sandwich to satisfy it that day. She was more ravenous than ever. Richard was right, she did often forget to eat when working on a murder case. Jane was always the one to order sandwiches or pick up lunch for her lest she go the entire day without a meal. When the waiter came to take her order she paired it with a selection from the red wine menu.

"I told them our theory about the *supposed* siblings," Kitty said.

"*Our* theory?"

"We both discussed it," she said, as though that was explanation enough. "I told them how we both agreed it was unusual to meet anyone from Norway, thus creating the perfect cover."

"Yes, yes, the nefarious Norwegians," Benny said before offering a tauntingly pursed mouth.

"I know several people of Norwegian descent," Richard said.

"What if they aren't even Norwegian?" Kitty insisted.

"Why would they pretend to be an entirely different nationality?" Cousin Cordelia asked, looking at Kitty with concern, as though that was confirmation of their wickedness.

As if on cue, Gustav and Elsa appeared. Their entrance didn't garner as much attention as Penelope's entrance had. After all, no one else had any reason to connect them to the murders. As such, they earned nothing more than idle glances at the new faces.

The pair were seated not too far from Penelope's table. At their continued gawking, Elsa in particular turned to give them a direct look, as though her public appearance should shut down all lingering gossip about the Norwegian siblings.

"Cousin, why don't you tell me about your activities today," Pen suggested, tactfully bringing everyone's attention back to their own table.

She wasn't immune from the same curiosity infecting the others, but manners were manners, even in the wake of murder. Still, while Cousin Cordelia lamented the lack of eligible partners for the dance class she had attended, Penelope considered Lulu's suggestion that the Norwegians weren't in fact siblings. Other than the similar fair hair coloring, they didn't look much alike. For example, Elsa's mouth was an upside-down image of Gustav's, with her bottom lip plumper than the top. Her brow was regular, eyebrows a much darker shade of blond than her hair. Her face was oval to his square.

Gustav had understandably taken a protective stance as he escorted Elsa in. Yes, his hand had been more intimately on the small of her back rather than mid- or higher. Perhaps that was a Norwegian habit?

"What are you thinking?" Kitty asked, staring hard at her, when there was a pause in Cousin Cordelia's talking.

"I'm thinking we should enjoy our soup," she replied, noting the waiter was conveniently arriving with said course.

"We were told about your adventures today," Benny hinted once the soup was served.

"That poor Edwin Pembrook," Cousin Cordelia lamented.

"So you think it was Hugo from the bar who has been hiding Marie this entire time?" Lulu asked.

"According to both Léa and Marc, he was quite smitten with her. Marc, a fellow bartender, claimed she may have had him quite under her spell. Besides, men love to play the hero, especially to a girl they are interested in." She smiled at Richard.

"Perhaps he discovered she was just using him and he got upset?" Lulu said.

Pen slowly shook her head in thought. "The timing is too coincidental. He's been hiding her for almost two weeks and just now, he is angry enough to kill her? It has to be related to Vivian's murder."

"Maybe he figured out she murdered Vivian and got upset about it."

"So he murders her?" Benny asked, looking skeptical.

Pen was suddenly distracted by Elsa rising from her chair to head to the ladies' room. As she went, she made direct eye contact with her, capturing her attention in a meaningful way. There was a message there to follow her. Pen broke the connection before anyone else noted it.

"If you'll excuse me," she said, hoping she wasn't too obvious as she quickly escaped to the ladies' room as well to find out what Elsa wanted to discuss.

CHAPTER TWENTY-FOUR

As expected, Elsa was waiting for Penelope in the ladies' room attached to the dining room. She joined her on one of the soft ottomans in the sitting area outside of where the toilets were located.

Elsa didn't waste time with niceties. "You're looking into this murder? I see they announced a second one, Marie Blanchet." There wasn't even a hint of the accent Gustav had. In fact, she sounded like an American, maybe from Boston. That certainly leaned in favor of them not being siblings.

"Yes. I believe Marie killed Vivian." Elsa's eyes widened in surprise. "I'm now trying to find out who killed Marie. I suspect it's related."

Elsa nodded. Pen waited for her to speak.

"Gustav is not my brother," she said after a moment.

"My friends and I guessed as much."

She offered a subdued smile and nodded. "He is my husband. Well, he soon will be."

"Why is that such a scandal?"

Elsa paused. "I come from a...complicated family environment. I met Gustav when he attended Harvard. I lived in Cambridge at the time." She paused to loosen her jaw, which had reflexively hardened in either anger or resentment. "My only escape was to take walks through Cambridge Common, it's the rare bit of nature you'll find there. That's how I met him. We were both staring at the same nest of baby robins. He was..." She smiled fondly. "He was the first boy I'd met who thought I had something worth saying."

A frown came to her face. "My family is quite religious, you see. Odd, as my father teaches—" she stopped suddenly, looking at Penelope in alarm.

"He teaches at Harvard? Let me guess, something in the sciences?"

Elsa swallowed hard, sitting so rigid Pen worried about her spine. She stayed like that for a moment, until she seemed to realize Penelope was waiting for the part of the story that necessitated such a reaction. She relaxed, and briefly closed her eyes.

"He teaches chemistry, yes at Harvard. I suppose it doesn't matter to reveal that now. Suffice it to say, I left an impossible situation. One where a life other than humble obedience to a husband was my only option. Gustav, he offered me a solution. I knew I wanted to marry him, and when the opportunity came, he finally returned for me. I'm going to live with him in Norway."

Pen's brow wrinkled in confusion. "Then who came with him to New York?"

"His sister. She has an independent mind, like me. But her options are more plentiful. Their family is not like mine. She wanted to come to America to study, like her older brother did. She'll be starting at Barnard College soon." There was a bitter twist to her mouth as she mentioned this.

Pen suspected college was out of the question for her, even a woman's college such as Radcliffe, Harvard's sister school.

"Why did she hide herself on the trip to New York? And why go through France?"

Elsa studied Pen, as though wondering how much to say. "Elsa did that for my sake, while Gustav slept on the sofa in the sitting room. She is like that, though, up for a bit of adventure. She actually laughed at how well she pulled it off. She told me even the maid never saw her—she'd hide in the bathroom when she came. She felt I deserved to be the one to show my face, enjoy my freedom. I had to dye my hair a much lighter shade of blonde to match hers.

"As for France? There will be people looking for me. My father had already chosen a husband for me, you see. He knew about Gustav, and he'd have men waiting for us at the port as soon as we arrived. Me posing as Elsa? I'd have to return to America right away. I said my family is religious; that doesn't just mean going to church every Sunday and saying grace before meals. They have a view toward women that doesn't align with the way things are today. They also have sects in every country, including Norway. Southern France was safer. We'll get married there and return to Norway when it's safe. When he assumes I've perhaps just run away somewhere in America. By then, it will be too late for him to do anything about it."

Penelope didn't have the best relationship with her own father, who was quite strict. Still, she couldn't imagine him being that controlling. Poor Elsa must have grown up in the equivalent of a prison.

Which begged the question... "What is your real name?"

She paused, a flicker of fear coming to her eyes before

she answered. "Eva. Conveniently similar enough to Elsa's name."

No last name, but perhaps that didn't matter.

"Elsa and I look enough alike from a distance, especially with my hair dyed, but anyone would be able to tell that she wasn't me if they'd met her. The only perilous time was boarding and departing, particularly for me as I'm traveling under her name. But now we're safely in international waters. None of the crew or staff ever saw Elsa up close, Gustav and Elsa both assured me."

"Vivian saw Elsa, enough to tell you have different body shapes."

"Did she?" Eva asked, unconvincingly.

"She did."

"I didn't kill her. You just said you think Marie did."

"Yes, but someone killed Marie. She presumably blackmailed Vivian. Who is to say she didn't do the same with Gustav and Elsa, now you?"

"I would never have killed over this. I may not agree with all the religious teachings I grew up with, but I still believe murder is a sin. What is the point in starting a life with Gustav based on the worst of all sins?" Eva seemed perfectly perplexed that Pen would even suggest a thing. "Besides, Gustav would have paid for her silence. Oftentimes, that's all it takes. His family has a shipping business. They've recovered well since the war when they nearly lost everything and had to make do. They're almost to the point they were before it began. Enough that Gustav could certainly pay whatever a maid might be asking for."

That much was certainly true. Based on what little Pen knew about Marie from others, she would have been far more interested in money than spreading gossip or revealing their secret to the proper authorities. And if Gustav could afford First Class tickets both coming and going, then he certainly would have had enough money to pay off Marie.

Eva's face quickly softened into something pleading as she focused on Pen. "I'm trusting you with this information, Miss Banks. I know you have no reason to keep this to yourself, but I'm begging you to. Gustav, Elsa, and I have done nothing wrong other than try to seek a better life for ourselves. That shouldn't be a criminal thing. I would certainly never commit cold-blooded murder."

"I suppose I can keep this to myself for now."

"Thank you, that's all I ask." Eva reached over unexpectedly and took both of Pen's hands to squeeze in gratitude.

Someone entered and Eva quickly let go and rose to leave. Penelope remained there for a moment, replaying the conversation in her head. She had no reason not to believe everything Eva had said and it made sense that she and Gustav would want to avoid scrutiny. Hence their odd behavior.

With nothing but soup currently in her stomach, Penelope didn't have the energy to think about it too much. Perhaps after dessert. She rose to leave and rejoin her table, where the main course was finally being served.

"Well?" Kitty was the first to ask—naturally. Penelope's departure coinciding with Eva's hadn't gone unnoticed. Frankly, she was surprised Kitty had maintained enough self-control not to follow them in.

"We told her she wasn't allowed to follow you," Richard explained, reading her mind.

"There is nothing to report. However, I do have even less reason to think either of them murdered Marie." She cast a quick look toward their table, and Eva met her eyes, flashing a brief smile before turning her attention back to

Gustav. Penelope then darted her eyes to the noticeably empty table next to them.

"I assume Simone is dining in her room." Pen didn't blame her. Most of the passengers had no idea Marie was the most likely suspect in Vivian's murder, which still made Simone a likely suspect in their eyes.

"Yes, I was thinking we should talk to her as well," Kitty said. "She must know what secret Vivian was keeping. The one that Marie was using for blackmail."

"Why don't we move on from the topic of murder?" Lulu suggested, easily sensing Penelope's state of mind.

"The library had a nice selection," Richard offered. It was amusingly banal in comparison, but she appreciated his attempt.

As she tucked into her roast beef, Pen felt a renewed sense of purpose. Perhaps Kitty was right, talking to Simone would be a good thing.

CHAPTER TWENTY-FIVE

After dinner, Kitty had feigned tiredness and excused herself back to her cabin. Everyone else had suggested going to the bar for nightcaps, even Cousin Cordelia, surprisingly. Penelope made the excuse of going to retrieve something from her room.

"So you want to join me in questioning Simone after all," Kitty said with a knowing laugh.

"I want to keep you from making a mess of things."

"I only seek the truth, as always. My journalistic integrity demands that I—"

"Oh stick a pin in that insect, Kitty, you're just nosy," Pen said with a laugh.

Kitty feigned a hurt look, then laughed as well. "As though a tiny part of you isn't as well."

"The truth is, we're running out of suspects, at least among the passengers. You and I can at least do more...*prodding* at this level than most of the staff can, even security. They're bound to be too deferential. Raul had a point about being an easy scapegoat from Third Class. Until I know for sure that he's been released, I'm not giving up. If it turns out to be someone in the crew who killed Marie, then I'll leave it to them to investigate. I'd certainly never use my position to be that intrusive. I feel no such reserve when it comes to Simone."

"And you're just as nosy as me," Kitty sang.

Penelope left that alone as they walked down the hallway for the First Class cabins and suites. They ended up in front of Simone's suite, right next to Vivian's, which was no longer guarded, but certainly locked. Pen cast a quick look that way, thinking about what happened a little less than twenty-four hours prior. A wave of sadness overcame her at the thought. Whatever Vivian's sins, it hardly warranted murder. At least Penelope hoped so.

She steeled herself and reached up to firmly knock on Simone's door. There was no response at first, which was expected, but when it went on for a full minute, she and Kitty eyed each other. Kitty was the one to knock again, harder this time. Again, there was no immediate response.

"Maybe she isn't—"

They both jumped when Simone opened the door. She sported a cool look on her face, as though she wasn't surprised to see either of them. One brow rose in a questioning manner, forcing them to explain themselves.

"We had a few questions," Kitty said, the directness in her tone making it seem more of a demand than a request. It didn't cause even a stir in Simone's marble facade.

"We've discovered who may have killed Vivian," Penelope explained. That earned them a twitch of curiosity. She narrowed her eyes at Penelope, as though wondering if she was telling the truth.

"Who?"

"Perhaps we could explain inside?"

Simone exhaled a quiet, cynical laugh. "This is a trap, no?"

"It isn't. You don't have to tell us a thing. It's your choice." Next to her, Penelope could sense Kitty stir with irritation.

"Very well," Simone said. Without another word, she turned around and walked further into her suite. Pen and Kitty briefly glanced at one another again, then shrugged and entered after her.

Simone was already seated on the couch in her sitting room, her back as erect as a ballerina's. That graceful stance and her beauty made Pen sharply aware of why Vivian may have felt reluctant to work with her. She and Kitty took the cushioned chairs across from her.

"Who killed her?"

"I think it was Marie Blanchet."

A slight crease of puzzlement touched Simone's pristine brow. "Why would she do that?"

"We're hoping you could tell us."

A flash of alarm and suspicion melted some of the ice in her gaze. "What is it you think I know?"

"Is there anything you can tell us about Vivian? We think it was a case of blackmail. Marie knew something about Vivian and when her scheme to get money didn't work out, she went into hiding, perhaps pretending to be dead so that she wouldn't face the consequences. Or perhaps she was in fear for her life."

The sides of Simone's mouth hitched up just a tad, as though wryly amused by that theory. "Vivian wasn't the darling everyone thinks she is, the lovely nightingale. Yes, she could charm anyone, but if you crossed her, she was—I think the phrase is 'scorched earth?'"

"And you crossed her?" Kitty asked, eyes glittering at the whiff of scandal.

Simone shot her a withering look. "I did not. In fact, I tried my best to endear myself to her. At first, it seemed to work. The first few weeks, during rehearsal she was lovely. Then...something changed. It was like turning a switch, she was irritable and snappish. No one knew why. And then...."

Kitty and Penelope waited, watching as Simone looked off to the side, anger blazing in her expression as she mentally recalled everything. When she turned back to them, the ice she used as a shield had shattered.

"I know someone was sabotaging me. My costume missing or damaged. Death notes that would appear, then disappear, telling me to quit the play, or else. When my understudy suddenly had an accident, I received a phone call telling me I was next. I only suspected her, because all of this happened so soon after she changed. I made the mistake of accusing her. By then I was a mess, everyone assumed I was hysterical." She was fiercely angry now. "I had to apologize to her, it was the most humbling experience of my life. Still, she insisted on postponing the play, taking a break to go to America. Of course, Pierre happily agreed.

"It was his idea for me to follow her, earn her trust again. He even persuaded the producers to pay for a First Class suite, for me to be as close as possible to her." Simone coughed out a laugh. "When she saw I was on the boat with her, she looked as though she wanted to kill me." Simone arched an eyebrow at the irony. "She accused me of snooping, stalking her to seek my revenge. I explained why I was here, falling over myself to beg her forgiveness. Then as soon as we were off, *voilà*, another switch. She was as nice as could be, insisting I join her every night at dinner even. That's when I knew for certain she had been the one to sabotage me. I can not tell you how I knew, I just did. Of course, I wasn't about to make the same mistake of accusing her again, not without proof. But I wasn't going to be sweet as sugar anymore."

"It seems perhaps Marie was the one to find proof, of something at least," Kitty suggested.

Simone shrugged as though she had no idea what that proof was.

"Do you have any idea what could have caused the change in her back in France?" Pen asked.

Simone shrugged again and shook her head.

"Try to remember. At the time, did she receive any mail or packages? Like you, perhaps she got phone calls or notes? Any visitors? Anything special happening at the time?"

"Not that I can recall."

"Think, Simone. It could be anything, something that may be meaningless to you, but not to her. Just tell us every-thing happening at the time."

Simone sighed and thought about it. "It was the same as usual. Rehearsal was fine. Joel Bernstein invited the cast and crew to Le Dôme, a café in Montparnasse. He did that often though, usually to some café on the *Rive Gauche*." Simone rolled her eyes, apparently not a fan of the artist set in the Left Bank. "Vivian went often enough to make people feel she was one of them. The next day, after that night at Le Dôme, she had changed. I asked Sara, one of the cast who went with them, and she said nothing had really happened at the café, save for Vivian leaving earlier than usual. The day after that, my costume went missing."

When Penelope had last spent time in Paris, the Left

Bank had only just become popular with Americans. She'd still had the veneer of elitism keeping her firmly among the wealthy American families who limited themselves to cafés along the Rue Scribe or Rue de la Paix.

"Is there anything special about Le Dôme?"

Simone lifted one shoulder in a shrug, but Pen noted the slight wrinkle of distaste in her nose. "It is popular with Eastern Europeans, Germans, Jews, Scandinavians, and such."

"Scandinavians?" Pen and Kitty both stated at the same time.

"And Americans of course," Simone said hesitantly, taken aback by their excited utterance. She obviously hadn't become acquainted with her neighbors the way Vivian had.

This news certainly pushed the arrow back in the direction of Gustav and Eva as somehow involved in all of this. Penelope couldn't for the life of her imagine how. She wanted to make sure she covered every possibility before turning her investigation back toward them.

"What about on the voyage to New York? That was presumably when Marie learned something about Vivian and tried to blackmail her. Did you notice any other change in her, beyond being nicer to you?"

"A few days before we docked, she fell on the stairs and injured her shoulder. Just moving it caused pain that first day. She begged my help for trifle tasks like picking things up, positioning items so she could use her left hand instead of her right hand—"

"Getting dressed," Penelope interjected.

Simone nodded. "Of course, I didn't help her with that. It's a maid's duty."

"So it's something Marie saw while Vivian was undressed." Kitty said excitedly, remembering how Vivian had mentioned needing her help the night before. "A scar? Birthmark? Tattoo?"

Simone shrugged. "I have never seen her undressed."

"But Marie certainly did," Penelope said. "And so did someone else on board, someone who is still alive."

CHAPTER TWENTY-SIX

PENELOPE QUICKLY THANKED SIMONE FOR HER TIME and grabbed Kitty to leave her suite.

"So do you speak from experience?" Kitty asked her with a teasing grin. "Did Raul paint you in the, *ahem*, altogether as well?"

"I regret nothing," Pen said blandly.

Kitty pursed her lips, upset she hadn't gotten more of a reaction. "Interesting about Le Dôme, though."

"It's a coincidence, and a rather tenuous connection to our Scandinavians."

"You really want to save those crazy Swedes, don't you?" Kitty said with a chuckle.

"They're not Swedish Kitty, they're Norwegian."

"So they say."

"Zounds, Kitty, you do come to the most absurd conclusions! I have to wonder if the *New York Register* is a legitimate paper if they give you any inches of ink."

"I check my sources and my facts." Kitty frowned with indignation.

"Never mind that, we need to talk to Raul."

Penelope led Kitty to the stairs and took them up to the First Class public area, then to the security office. The two new security officers at the desk both instantly recognized Penelope and she could see guarded looks come to both their faces.

"Mademoiselle Banks," David greeted in a wary tone. "Do you have something to report?"

He'd been the one Léa had charmed over the phone, so Penelope plastered on a coquettish smile. "I urgently need to talk to Raul again."

"Why?" He narrowed his eyes with suspicion.

"He may provide an important clue to the murders."

"What clue is that?" His interest was instantly piqued.

"That's what I need to ask him."

The two men looked at one another, silently communicating, before David turned back to Pen. "Monsieur García has been released. He is back in the Third Class passenger level."

"Well that's good news," she said, pleased. Something else occurred to her. "You haven't arrested poor Hugo, the bartender, have you? Someone mentioned he had been removed from his post in the bar."

Both their mouths tightened with displeasure, obviously annoyed by how quickly news spread on the ship. "What do you know of Hugo?"

"Only that he was escorted from his post. Surely you don't think he killed Marie?" Now that she'd posed the questions, she couldn't discount it herself. After all, crimes of passion were called that for a reason. Still, she wanted to note their reactions to see if she was onto something.

"Mademoiselle Banks," David said, his eyes flitting to Kitty behind her. He probably knew she was a reporter.

"Please trust that we are making every effort to ensure the safety of our passengers."

Jean spoke up, looking anxious. "Perhaps Monsieur Duval is better equipped to—"

"Thank you!" Pen said, quickly grabbing Kitty and exiting the security office. The last thing she wanted was an audience with Alfred, who would waste time with more questions.

Penelope wanted answers first.

They sprinted down to the Third Class level. It wasn't until they arrived that she realized she had no idea which cabin Raul was in. They were so plentiful down there that even knocking on each door would waste time.

"There has to be a way that we can find him."

"Didn't Vivian say something about him sneaking up to other class levels? He may be on the upper decks this very moment," Kitty said.

"I doubt he would break the rules so quickly after being released."

"So how should we find him?"

Penelope thought about it, then it came to her. "We have him come to us. And at the same time learn more about a suspect I've had yet to interrogate."

Before Kitty could ask what she meant, Pen had her quickly chasing to catch up as she returned to the First Class level.

"Where are we going?" Kitty protested as they went up several floors to the First Class public areas.

"To the bar."

"But we're still in our dinner clothes!"

"Kitty," Pen said in exasperation, stopping to stare down at her on the steps below. "I never took you as one for decorum when there is a story to be had. We're on the cusp of solving two murders and you're worried about a party dress."

Kitty's mouth protruded a bit. "Don't be silly. Of course this is more important. I just wish you'd tell me what is going on in that zany head of yours."

"You'll see."

When Penelope arrived at the Clair de Lune, she was surprised to see it so full. Perhaps the air of danger or grief had people turning to their cups. The jazz band did their part, luring far too many people to the dance floor with an upbeat tune to shimmy their troubled minds away. Pen had an idea there were far more people here than had taken the ship's chaplain up on his offer to console them.

She found the rest of their group seated at the same table they were at the night before when Vivian had asked them to join her. Even Cousin Cordelia seemed to have gotten over her reluctance to publicly drink. It no doubt helped that the ever reliable Detective Prescott was sitting right next to her enjoying his own drink. Pen admired him all the more for being her cousin's reliable rock, though it made her plans rather tricky.

Benny was the first to greet them, his eyes narrowing with suspicion. "And just where have you two trouble-makers been?"

"Solving two murders while you all drink the night away," Kitty answered, getting her claws in right away.

"You found out who killed Marie?" Cousin Cordelia exclaimed.

"No, we didn't," Pen said, giving Kitty a scolding look. She turned back to the others. "But we may be close to finding a motive."

"How so?" Richard asked.

Pen took a breath before addressing him. "I think Raul

may have inadvertently discovered Vivian's secret. Or at least he may give us a clue as to what Marie may have discovered. I plan on talking to him."

She waited for him to utter a protest or frown with disapproval, but was surprised by his instant, unconditional response.

"If you need to talk to him, talk to him."

"We do," Pen said, pleased to see him so accommodating.

"Did you think I would be opposed to it?" One side of his mouth hitched up. "My only concern has been your safety, Penelope."

Now it was her turn to twitch her mouth. "Oh really? So you were *never* bothered by Raul?"

"Pen, honey, if you don't stop teasing your man..." Lulu scolded across from them with a laugh. "Don't you dare make him admit he was jealous in the middle of all that's going on."

Richard lifted his glass toward Lulu, then turned to grin at Penelope.

"Oh stop already," Benny said waving a hand in the air. "If it means seeing Raul again, let's get to it. What's the next step, dove?"

"Well," Penelope craned her head, searching the crowded bar until she found the person she was looking for. "There."

Gerard had a decidedly strained smile on his face that evening. He no longer had to table hop to greet the First Class passengers. Instead, they seemed to flock to him like, well, like ducks. Pen could see them squawking out their questions and pecking him for more information.

When he saw Penelope approaching, the smile on his face cracked. He couldn't mask the alarm in time for her to miss it, but Pen didn't let it deter her. She cut through the passengers crowding him, such that he had no choice but to address her.

"Mademoiselle Banks, how are you this evening?" The smile on his face was so forced, Pen thought he might hurt himself.

"I wondered if I could ask a small favor."

He blinked once, the smile freezing, before he answered. "Oh?"

"If I wanted to get a message to someone in Third Class, or better yet, invite them up to join me in First Class, say for dinner or a drink, how would I go about doing that?"

He frowned, staring at her as though wondering if there was some trouble she might be brewing up. Perhaps he was mentally weighing the risks of accommodating her. After all, Pen hadn't ruled him out as a suspect.

Gerard seemed to realize they had an audience. Enough people around them had seen that Penelope was involved in the aftermath of Vivian's death to now find her an object of curiosity. They were no doubt mentally putting that together with her request and wondering what relation it had to either death.

"It's quite loud in here, Mademoiselle Banks. Why don't we discuss this elsewhere so I can better accommodate you." Without waiting for an answer, he gently placed a hand on her back to escort her out of the bar.

"Here, that's better," he said, his eyes darting around to make sure they were alone. The facade dropped and he studied her with a look of uncertainty still etched in his features. That pale pencil mustache twitched before he continued. "There are strict boundaries between Third Class and First Class, I'm afraid."

"Yes, however, Miss Adler was able to get Raul García

into the First Class dining room. Perhaps I could be afforded the same accommodation? It wouldn't even be for a meal. I simply need to talk with him. At the very least, perhaps I could find out his cabin number so I could talk with him down in Third Class."

Gerard seemed horrified by at least one of those ideas, Penelope wasn't sure which one.

"Naturally, we want to accommodate every request from our First Class passengers. I will instantly have a page sent down to invite Monsieur García up. Was there anything else you needed?"

"Actually, yes." Again the look of panic appeared, quickly snuffed out as he planted a polite questioning smile on his face. "Hugo, one of the bartenders. I noticed he wasn't working tonight. I wanted to thank him for the wonderful martini he made. Is there a way to have him sent up as well?"

"I apologize, but I'm afraid that won't be possible. Hugo is...he is indisposed."

"Have they arrested him?"

Gerard winced, his eyes darting back and forth. "Please, Mademoiselle Banks," he hissed in a whisper. "There are certain things not to be discussed in public."

She'd have to pick her battles. Right now, she needed Raul. Hugo could come later, once she had learned more.

"Please just see to Raul, if you could. I'd like to speak to him as soon as possible."

"Of course," he said, back to his obsequious role. He hesitated before adding. "Perhaps it would be best for you to wait here for him."

Penelope didn't argue. In fact, that was preferable. Too many people had seen Raul with Vivian at dinner, and he would draw too much attention in the bar. An added benefit was that none of her friends would interfere.

Still, Pen wasn't surprised when, after ten minutes, Richard exited to join her. She was even a bit pleased to see him.

"Worried we had run off together?" Penelope teased.

"I admit I'm jealous. Are you happy?"

"Rather," she said with a grin and a twitch of the nose.

They both laughed softly. At least until Gerard returned, personally escorting Raul. When he saw Penelope, a broad smile came to his face. He completely ignored Richard.

"Penelope, thank you! Gracias, mi am—" He stopped short, eyeing Richard and then taking Pen's hands and kissing the backs of them. "The painting is yours. Anything, now that I am free."

She didn't want to waste time explaining that it hadn't been her doing that had liberated him. She assumed Alfred had found the towels or smelled the gunpowder on Marie's gloves. Also, Penelope didn't want to give him a reason not to give her the painting.

"I have a question for you, Raul."

Gerard stepped away, but she stopped him. "Actually, I think you should hear this as well."

Penelope wanted to gauge his reaction to anything said. Gerard didn't seem the type to easily hide his emotions, and she was waiting to see any indication of guilt or fear on his face in reaction to Raul's answers.

"Of course."

Now that she had the attention of all three men, she hesitated, realizing how delicate the topic was. Then she remembered Kitty's suggestion about being direct. "Did Vivian pose without clothes for your painting?"

Gerard inhaled sharply. Richard eyed Penelope with a curious look. Penelope ignored them both in favor of Raul.

A subtle, perplexed smile touched Raul's mouth. "*Claro que sí.* Of course."

"Did you notice any distinguishing marks?"

"No."

"Was there anything that you saw? Any scar or mark?" Pen asked, feeling disheartened that perhaps she was going down entirely the wrong road.

"Well...she wore makeup."

"I imagine so," Pen said with a sharp laugh, realizing this was a fruitless endeavor. "Even I wore makeup."

"No, I mean, on her back."

"To cover something up?" Richard was the one to ask.

"Yes." Raul reached around to his lower right back to show them where. "It was here. I only saw it because the red scarf she was draped in smeared some of it. You know red is my signature color." He grinned at Penelope.

She ignored his need to flirt now of all times. "What did the makeup cover?"

"A tattoo."

"Really?" Pen said, scandalized. She had never person-ally known a woman with a tattoo. Frankly, she didn't know many men who had them. The rare occasions she'd seen them on women had been at carnivals or wandering particu-larly unsavory areas of a city. Someone of Vivian's stature having one was quite shocking.

"What was it a tattoo of?" Richard asked.

"A bird."

"A nightingale?" Pen said, thinking of Vivian's nickname.

Raul shook his head. "It was black, like...a crow or the other one."

"A raven?" Pen's eyebrows pinched together in confusion.

Raul nodded. "With some words underneath; I could not see those very well. I told her to let me include it. She had said she wanted a memento, something to look back on fondly when she was older, while she still looked as she did now, you see."

"Why would she have a raven tattooed on her?" Pen asked in wonder. "Anyone who heard a nightingale and a raven would know one of those is a songbird and the other is, well, just noise. Quite disruptive."

"She insisted I leave it out; that I not tell anyone about it. I would have never, but I told her youth is nothing if not flawed, no? One day it would be fun to show people how daring she had been, especially as time goes by." He shrugged. "She was not interested. That was when she claimed to be too tired to continue."

In other words, she wanted Raul to stop discussing it, Pen thought. She was probably appalled he had seen it. But how did that lead to Marie first blackmailing her, then murdering her? Having a tattoo alone was daring, but hardly damning. If anything, the rumors of it would have created an interesting mystique about her.

The tattoo obviously had meaning. No one got a tattoo on a lark. Perhaps it was the meaning behind it that Vivian didn't want to become public. But Marie had figured it out.

"We need to see what the words underneath it were." Penelope turned to Gerard, who looked lost in some thought. His brow was furrowed and he muttered something incoherent to himself.

"Monsieur Canard?" Pen waited for him to snap back to attention, but it was as though the rest of them weren't there. "*Gerard?*"

That got his attention, and he blinked rapidly before focusing on Penelope. "Oui, yes, what is it?"

"We need to speak to Alfred Duval."

Rather than answer, he turned to Raul, studying him hard for some reason. He swallowed, then nodded. "Of course. Please come with me."

Penelope turned to look at Richard. The way he looked back at her meant he had seen Gerard's odd reaction as well. She saw Raul studying both of them, a sad smile on his face. He quickly erased it and turned to follow Gerard ahead of them.

CHAPTER TWENTY-SEVEN

"WE NEED THE DOCTOR ON BOARD TO CHECK VIVIAN'S tattoo," Penelope said once Gerard had taken her, Richard, and Raul down to the security office.

Alfred blinked twice at the mention of a tattoo, no doubt just as surprised to learn someone like Vivian had one. His gaze flitted to Gerard, who was still lost in some thought. There was a flash of irritation at his lack of attention.

"You think this tattoo has meaning?" Alfred, as usual, looked skeptical. He again eyed Gerard, who was only half paying attention. Pen was desperate to know what was weighing so heavily on his mind, but her priority at the moment was that tattoo.

"I assume the doctor has at least done a preliminary examination of the body, if only to determine it was the gunshot that killed her?" Richard interjected.

Alfred nodded.

"We only need to know what is written underneath the tattoo of a raven on her lower back," Penelope said.

"Monsieur Canard? Perhaps you have something to contribute?" Alfred said with a hint of exasperation.

Gerard slowly brought his attention back to everyone surrounding him. "I...I may know what Marie discovered."

Everyone in the office was suddenly more alert.

"What is it?" Alfred demanded.

"Night Raven." He ignored their blank looks and continued to explain. "It was Mademoiselle Banks who made me think of it: nightingale. Then Monsieur García said it was a raven. The tattoo, that must have been her verification, how her conspirators identified her."

"What are you talking about?" Alfred said, looking as perplexed as the rest of them.

"In the war, I worked with intelligence. I speak five languages fluently," he said solemnly, a note of pride coloring his voice. "There were rumors of a woman working as a spy for the Germans. She ingratiated herself with high-profile officers, British and French, learning more, then sending that information to someone in the German military. No one knew if it was some simple prostitute or a socialite. But Mademoiselle Adler?" His brow furrowed in bewilderment. "C'est impossible!"

Penelope recalled Simone's comment about Vivian being popular with the troops during the war. Vivian hadn't even blinked in response. She really had been quite the actress.

Alfred turned to one of his men. "Please get Doctor Granger, now!" The officer quickly left and he turned his attention back to Gerard. "Tell me everything you know about this Night Raven."

Gerard fell into the seat the officer had vacated, looking as though he had been personally blindsided by Vivian. "It was mostly in the north, sabotaging ships in the English

Channel. Messages were intercepted. Resources stolen or destroyed. Many men killed. She is responsible for it all!" Now he looked angry.

Alfred looked almost as incensed. Penelope could understand why. She thought of all the boys she knew who had been killed, even in the short amount of time America had been involved in the Great War. There would have been far more losses among the French.

It would have been the perfect thing with which to blackmail Vivian Adler.

The security officer returned with the ship's doctor, who stared at everyone in the room with a puzzled expression.

"Doctor Granger, you found a tattoo on the body of Vivian Adler?"

"*Oui,*" he said nodding.

"There was a word or phrase underneath a bird?"

He nodded again. "Yes, a raven I believe. The words were German I suspect, 'immer lieben'?"

"Love always," Gerard said with a sneer, as though repulsed at such a tender sentiment tattooed on such a devious woman.

"She mentioned something about falling in love with the wrong man," Penelope said. "Perhaps he was a German officer who coerced her into—"

"Non!" Gerard interrupted, suddenly full of outrage. "You will not excuse her actions!"

Penelope decided to move on to another topic. "We need to speak with Hugo. Find out how Marie knew what Vivian's tattoo meant."

Alfred's eyes darted around the room, focusing mostly on Penelope, Richard, and Raul. She was ready to argue how their presence might be beneficial. All of them had some bit of information that, when combined, would only help discover the truth. Fortunately, he came to that conclusion on his own.

"Please get Hugo," he said to the same officer who had retrieved the doctor.

They waited in silence, all of them absorbing the discovery of Vivian Adler's secret. She really had been quite the wolf in sheep's clothing.

Penelope thought about what Simone had said about her sudden transformation after a night at Le Dôme, the bar patronized by Germans, among others. Had she run into a former German officer? Someone who knew who she was and what role she had played in the war? It was no wonder she wanted to escape Paris so soon after that. She had most likely been the one to terrorize Simone, in order to have a reason to leave.

The officer returned with Hugo, who looked as though he was ready for another round of verbal punishment. His brow wrinkled in confusion at the addition of the three passengers and doctor in the overly crowded security office.

"Hugo," Pen said, speaking up before everyone else. "Can you tell us why Marie may have killed Vivian? I assume you were the one hiding her while on board?"

His eyes slid to Alfred with uncertainty. "I already answered these questions."

"You can repeat them. Right now the truth is more important than any repercussions."

Hugo sighed, looking chagrined. "She didn't tell me about Vivian. I had no idea! I just knew she was scared. That night she disappeared, or pretended to; she said someone had tried to push her overboard. If not for two drunken passengers enjoying a late-night tryst on that particular deck at the last minute, she would be dead."

Again his eyes darted to Alfred before he continued. "She wanted me to hide her and I agreed. When her disappearance was discovered, we were all assigned to search the ship. Naturally, I hid her in the location I was assigned. It was not difficult. I brought her clean uniforms to wear—men's uniforms, so it would not be suspicious when I took them out. I didn't understand why she wanted gloves, but now I suppose I do. I could not get white gloves because of how they are sent to the launders. It was easy enough to get the long black gloves though.

"When I learned about the murder, I suspected it was her. When I confronted her, all she could talk about was how important it had been to protect herself, how she should be getting a medal for what she'd done."

Everyone in the office made eye contact with one another at that. Yes, she'd killed a spy, a traitor to the side Vivian's home country had fought for. Marie might have even had a case for self-defense, however weak.

"Did she tell you how she came about this information?" Pen asked.

He shook his head. "As I said, I did not even know it was Mademoiselle Adler she was blackmailing."

"But you knew it was blackmail?"

"Only after I hid her. By then it was mostly a matter of protecting her. If I'd known beforehand that was how she was getting the money she kept talking about, I would have tried to stop her."

"Did she give you any indication about how she knew Vivian's secret?" Pen asked. "Is there anything in her background that would have given her knowledge about it?"

He shrugged. "She is from Calais."

"That was the main point of departure for the British

soldiers," Richard said. "Most of them lingered there for quite a while. Long enough to get to know the locals."

"She worked in a bar," Hugo said. "It helped her practice her English, she said. That was why she thought she deserved to work in the bar on the ship. She was upset about that."

British soldiers in a bar. That was plenty of opportunity for loose lips. Perhaps mentioning a certain birdie who spilled secrets during the war. That must have been how she'd learned about the Night Raven.

"Was there anyone else on board she was afraid of?" Pen asked. "Do you have any idea who may have killed her?"

"No," he pleaded, his eyes landing on Alfred, who must have suspected him of the crime. "It wasn't me! I told her to turn herself in. I would support her claim that she feared for her life. Even after stealing the gun, she would probably only be fired for that, not go to prison. But she was insistent that she had another way to get money, that she had discovered someone else on board who would be willing to pay for the same information."

"The same information? Meaning what she had learned about Vivian?"

"I assume so. She wouldn't listen to me when I told her to just give up, especially after how close she came to death the first time."

"Someone obviously succeeded the second time," Richard said.

"Someone who wanted that information and wasn't willing to pay for it," Penelope said, turning to him. "Like perhaps the close relative of a soldier who was mysteriously killed in the war."

CHAPTER TWENTY-EIGHT

"What information do you have?" Alfred demanded, looking at both Richard and Penelope. "Do you know who killed Marie Blanchet?"

"We may," Pen answered. "The Pembrooks, George and Edwin. The oldest son, Edwin's brother, died in the Great War."

"Many people lost someone in the war."

"But how many also had Marie for a maid and shared a drink with Vivian?"

Alfred seemed to consider that, then came to a decision. "Thank you for your assistance. My team and I will handle this now."

"But—"

"I can no longer allow you to be involved. We will question the two gentlemen, thank you. Jules, please escort the passengers to their respective floors."

Jules offered a sympathetic look as he stood, gesturing for Penelope, Richard, and Raul to leave ahead of him. Pen sighed and exited the office first. Alfred was right, of course. She had no reason to be involved at this point.

Penelope was now certain it was either George or Edwin who had killed Marie. The anger of being so close to finding out what had happened to George Pembrook Jr. only to have Marie insist on payment first. It must have been infuriating. Enough to kill perhaps.

She resigned herself to the fact that at least she would eventually find out which of them had done it, if it was one of them. George seemed the most likely candidate. She couldn't imagine poor, sweet Edwin committing murder, but Kitty had been right when she said anyone was capable of it.

Jules escorted Raul to the door for the Third Class area. He didn't leave without one last goodbye to Penelope.

"Gracias, once again, Penelope. I consider our reunion to have been quite worth it." He took her left hand before she could stop him, and kissed the back of it. He pulled up only slightly, deliberately looked at her third finger and slid a sly smile Richard's way. He let go and spun around to return to his quarters.

"I suppose I should do something about that," Richard said, giving Pen a wry, unamused look.

"No pressure," she quipped.

Jules urged them on, up toward the First Class level, depositing them where she and Gerard had been earlier. Her friends were no doubt still in the bar, wondering what she and Richard had been up to this entire time.

"Let's go to the Salon for a moment. I'm not quite ready for a barrage of questions just now."

Richard nodded, taking her hand and leading her down the stairs to where the Soleil Salon was situated right beneath the bar. It was blessedly more peaceful there. At night, the low lighting from the lamps made it feel more intimate.

Which was presumably why George and Edwin were sitting there, having a rather animated private conversation. In fact, they were the only two people there at the moment.

Penelope stared in surprise, then turned to Richard.

"Penelope," Richard said in a warning tone.

"I'm not going to alert them security is looking for them. But if I can get them talking while they still have their guard down, I may be able to solve this murder, for the sake of everyone involved. A woman's delicate touch may just be the thing. You're too much of a detective, and anyone from security will just have them defensive."

Richard looked uncertain.

"Do you trust me?" She studied him, waiting for his answer.

"Just...be careful."

Pen smiled, then proceeded.

"Why hello, Edwin! What a pleasant surprise to find you here," Pen said, approaching them as though she had just noticed they were there.

The two instantly pulled away from one another, looks of surprise on their faces at the intrusion.

"And this must be your father," Pen said, offering a broad smile to George Sr. He didn't offer a welcoming smile in return. In fact, he looked ready to tell her to leave, so she quickly continued. "I was so sorry to hear about your son in the war. To die under such mysterious circumstances...."

George's expression instantly transitioned. He studied Penelope with a calculated look.

"Why the devil would you bring up my son?" His voice was dangerously calm.

Pen swallowed, feeling the animosity in the air. "I just... I apologize for interrupting." She turned to leave.

"You wait right there."

Pen stopped, turning back to George, who stood from his chair. He didn't see Richard behind him, slowly walking their way after noting the danger from afar.

"Father," Edwin said in a voice laced with concern.

"Quiet. You've done enough," George snapped. He turned to Penelope again. "What do you know about my son?"

"I..." Penelope stopped, narrowing her eyes with scrutiny as he came closer. "What have you done?"

Something flickered in his eyes, guilt or fear. That's when Penelope knew it had been George who killed Marie.

"Father, don't!" Edwin shouted, which only seemed to spur his father. George lunged for Penelope, but by then Richard was already there to grab him from behind. Having the advantage of both surprise and physicality, it was easy enough to restrain him, both arms pulled sharply behind his back.

Pen's heart was already in her throat and she forced it to return to normal. George struggled only a moment before realizing he had no chance against someone like Richard.

"What is going on!"

They all turned to see a woman wearing a black dress, heels, and long black gloves observing the scene with an expression of shock.

"Go and get security. Tell them we have Monsieur Pembrook here. Quickly!" Richard barked.

It startled her into action. She quickly left, her eyes wide with alarm.

"What did she mean, father? What did you do? Did you kill Vivian?"

"Shut up, Edwin!"

"Not Vivian, Marie," Penelope said.

"Marie? The pretty maid? Why would you do that?"

"You stupid boy," George seethed. "You have no idea. Flirting with silly shop girls and scheming maids. All the while she's holding onto information that could have told us everything! Your brother would have understood. He would have done the same thing!"

Security rushed in, hopefully having heard George all but confess. Richard handed him over to them, just as Alfred and the others entered the salon.

"I don't regret it," George snarled, now looking like a lunatic. "We could have learned everything. When she idly pulled off those silly gloves, as though she hadn't a care in the world. As though she wasn't holding onto information I've spent nearly the past ten years trying to learn. Then, asking for such an absurd amount, as though everything didn't hinge on that information. As though my son didn't deserve his proper justice! My only *real* son!"

Everyone stared in shock as he was taken away, everyone save for Edwin, who simply stared back at his father with a numb expression.

"I'm so sorry, Edwin," Penelope said, placing a hand on his shoulder.

He sank back into his chair. "He did it, he really killed her."

Twenty minutes had passed and Edwin still seemed to be in a daze. But he was certainly talking.

"I liked her." Edwin didn't stare at anyone in particular, even though Penelope, Richard, Alfred, and a few other members of the security team surrounded him.

Penelope had given him a brief summary of everything, explaining who Vivian was and the fact that Marie had most likely murdered her, then tried to sell the information to his father.

"Father is right, I have a weakness for girls like her. She

reminded me of Angela. She was good at listening; allowed me to blather on about myself. She was particularly interested in George, wanting to know more about him and what he'd done in the war." He coughed out a small laugh. "I suppose now I know why."

A glaze of clarity came to his eyes and he turned his attention to Penelope. "Do you think that's why Vivian wanted that drink with me? Because she knew about George? When I met her, I gave her my last name. I thought mentioning I'd be the future Earl of Greymoor would impress her.

Pen wasn't sure how to answer in a way that would make him feel better. That probably had been why she'd shown such an interest in him. But now, he'd lost both a beloved brother and a not-so-beloved father. His life would be forever changed once again.

"You don't have to answer," he said with a rueful smile. It disappeared with some dark thought that reflected in his eyes. "Is it terrible that I understand why he did it? If Vivian really is who you claim, the world should know about it. We should have been allowed to learn the truth directly from her. Father has always had a temper. Still, I never would have thought him capable of..." He couldn't finish the sentence.

"I know this must be a shock to you."

He exhaled sharply and fell back in his chair his eyes wide. "What am I to tell mother? Elizabeth? Violet? Margot?"

"I'm sure there are some people in authority who can inform your mother and sisters." She gave Alfred a questioning look.

"Rest assured, French Transatlantique will handle all these matters, Monsieur Pembrook."

Everyone was surprised when Edwin hiccuped a soft, cynical laugh.

"What is it, Edwin?" Pen asked, worried he might be going slightly mad.

"You know...I'm not even sure what happens when an earl is arrested for murder." He looked off to the side in thought. "I'd be happy if they tossed the whole damn title in the rubbish bin."

Penelope could certainly understand that sentiment. Just look at what that title had done for him in his short life. Absolutely nothing.

EPILOGUE

"It is actually quite a good painting," Richard said, a begrudging note of admiration in his voice as he stared at it.

The ship's crew had made special arrangements to retrieve Raul's painting from stowage so he could gift it to Penelope in the wake of everything that had happened with George Pembrook, who was presently occupying the same cell Raul had been in only a few days prior.

Telegrams had been wired. Passengers had been updated—withholding the name of the suspect in custody of course. Begrudging appreciation had been offered to Penelope and her friends by Alfred.

In the storm of it, the news had been privately conveyed to Richard and Penelope (and with strict instruction that it remain private) that a German man had been found murdered in the Left Bank only a week before the *Lumière-de-France* had taken off on its maiden voyage. Penelope suggested Alfred report back that they should check to see if he had been a patron at Le Dôme the night he was last seen.

Edwin had taken to his suite ever since his father was taken into custody. Penelope had tried knocking on his door, but he had understandably told her he wished to be left alone. It would take some time, but she felt he would do fine, perhaps even thrive now that his tyrannical father was no longer a presence in his life.

Now, she was in her suite with Richard and Raul staring at the painting he'd done of her. It looked exactly as Pen had remembered—of course it did. She could even picture herself posing for it as though it were yesterday.

Her back was to the viewer, her head turned in profile so anyone could recognize it was her. She was lounging on a window seat, twisted toward the view of the Mediterranean Sea beyond. A red scarf was draped just so, covering everything between her lower back and upper thighs.

It was tasteful.

It was art.

It was hers.

"As promised, Penelope, it is yours," Raul said, staring at the painting with a pained look on his face. Penelope observed him, studying that expression.

In response to her questions about Clifford Stokes' request to purchase the painting, he had been able to offer little of value. Raul wasn't even sure how he knew about it. There had simply been a telegram with an offered amount, the price too good to turn down. Penelope was just glad he had thought to sell it to her first, even if he had expected her to pay more for it.

It was something worth investigating at some point, but Penelope wasn't about to ruin her time in Europe by thinking about that man. Besides, the painting was hers now. Yet another disaster with Clifford thwarted at the last minute.

"Of course I'll still pay for it, Raul."

His eyes snapped to her in surprise. "Oh no. You saved me. I cannot accept payment."

"Applesauce. I only meddled, as usual. I wouldn't feel good about accepting it as a gift. The truth would have come out even without my help. I insist on paying you." She paused before tilting her head to consider him again. "Besides, something tells me you need this money?"

He flashed a smile before exhaling with far too much relief.

"What is it? Are you in trouble? Is that why you were in France not Barcelona?"

He viciously shook his head, and Penelope was surprised to see tears come to his eyes. "I was running away like a coward. There is a woman I was with in Barcelona. I thought I loved her, but when she...when she told me she was with child, I panicked. I fled to France to escape my obligations. Then, I received a telegram. It was a girl; her name is Sofia. *Mi dulce hija.*" He laughed with delight, swallowing it as he continued to explain. "That is why I was going to New York. This painting, it was one of only a few I still had. I knew you had money, having gone back home to your father. I did not know how much you now have, of course. But I thought you would be able to buy the painting. Then I would have money to provide for her—to be a father, and soon a husband, of course."

"Oh Raul, that's wonderful. Now I *have* to pay for it, of course. Enough for you to return to Barcelona and be a proper father *and* husband."

They went back and forth, congratulating and thanking one another. Just before Raul made his good-byes, he took Penelope's left hand once again to kiss the back of it. He pulled up and grinned at her third finger, then eyed Richard. "Do not wait too long, señor, she is a gem."

"No pressure," Richard said with a wry look once he'd left.

"None at all," Penelope said with a smirk, sauntering away.

Richard rushed over and grabbed her, pulling her in closer and taking her breath away.

"Richard!" Penelope exclaimed, laughing in surprise. It faded when she saw the look in his eyes.

"You *do* know that I want to marry you, don't you?"

She studied him. "Do you?"

"Of course." He stared in confusion. "You seem uncertain."

"I'm not, it's just..." She took a breath before continuing. "Does my rather significant wealth bother you? Is it too much?"

He laughed, thinking she was joking. It died when he realized she was serious. "Of course not, why would you think that?"

"Why didn't you arrive at the pier with the rest of us? You seem distant and troubled lately. Are you angry about what happened in that case with the Fabergé Egg? Do you blame me for your administrative leave?"

"Is that what has you worried?" He seemed incredulous, loosening his hold on her. He pulled away and led her to the sofa. Penelope braced herself, wondering what was coming. She wasn't sure if it was good news or bad.

"I have to confess something to you."

"What is it?" Pen felt a sense of dread overcome her.

"There is an ulterior motive for me joining you in Europe. Let me first make it clear, I wanted to join you. But once certain people learned I was going to Europe anyway, they made a request of me."

"Are you going to tell me what it is?"

"The egg. They suspect it's ended up somewhere in Europe. That's why I arrived to the ship later than expected. I was getting the latest information about it and who might have it. Suffice it to say, my detective hat isn't completely off during this trip."

Penelope breathed out in relief, allowing herself to relax. She laughed. "Is that all?"

"I didn't want to ruin your trip with the news. I thought I could operate without you knowing."

"Richard, why not use my help?"

"Shall I offer the usual reasons?"

"Now that I know, you have no choice, you realize? Besides, we work well as a team."

He studied her, a serious expression on his face.

"Is there something more?"

"You're absolutely right, my dear. I shouldn't have left you in the dark about what I'm involved in. I can't believe you thought I was angry or resentful. And just so you never have to wonder again..."

He sank to the floor on one knee in front of her.

"Richard?" Penelope felt her heart beat faster.

When he reached into his pocket and pulled out a box, she inhaled so sharply she nearly lost her breath.

"This isn't exactly how I'd planned on doing this, and I know we both said that we would mutually agree that we'd wait until—"

"Yes!"

Richard blinked. "You haven't even given me a chance to finish."

"I'm mutually agreeing to marry you." She frowned. "That is where you were going with this, wasn't it?"

"Yes, it was." He grinned. "After all, I can't have any more European Romeos from your past upstaging me."

Pen leaned in to drape her arms around his neck. "There's only one man I plan on ever...*endeavoring* with in the future, Detective Prescott."

He laughed, remembering their first encounter after their original case, another where they'd worked well as a team. He opened the box and Penelope gasped when she saw the ring inside. It was a gray pearl abutted on either end with two small jade insets.

"I had it specially made. I know how much jade means to you. Of course, if it isn't what you—"

"It's perfect," she cried.

Richard let out a small breath. "In which case, if I can finish, Penelope Banks, will you do me the honor of becoming my wife?"

"I will," she said, filled with glee.

He pulled the ring out and placed it on her finger. It fit perfectly and she held up her hand to admire it.

"How long have you had this?"

"A while now. Of course, I had to ask your father's permission first."

Pen tore her eyes away from her ring and stared at him with irritation.

"I don't want to hear it. There are some things that deserve adherence to tradition, this is one of them."

She pursed her lips. "I suppose I can forgive you for that," she teased.

Richard grinned. "Then again, there are other things that I'm more than happy to be quite modern about. We have yet to take advantage of the fact that there is no little orange-haired monster to intrude on us. That painting has given me some very newfangled ideas."

Richard stood and pulled Penelope up from the sofa. She laughed in surprise when he swiftly picked her up in his arms and carried her away.

"Let's *endeavor*, Miss Banks."

AUTHOR'S NOTE

As always, one of the joys of writing historical mysteries is the research. I'm an unapologetic francophile, and it only made sense that Penelope & Co. would travel to France as many Americans did during the 1920s. Stay tuned for those adventures. As such, they naturally took a French ocean liner.

FRENCH OCEAN LINERS

The *Lumière-de-France* is based on a combination of two ships that helped herald the age of French passenger ships, the S.S. Ile de France and later, the S.S. Normandie or "The Ship of Light." These were the first of the French liners to incorporate the new Art Deco style which had become popular during the Paris Exposition in 1925.

They were also quite liberated when it came to race, particularly if you had the money to travel First Class. There is an infamous story about A'Lelia Walker, the daughter of the Madam C. J. Walker first black female millionaire (and first self-made female millionaire) in America, who decided to travel the world. She set off aboard a French liner in 1921, occupying a First Class cabin next to French Prime Minister, Aristide Briand.

GET YOUR FREE BOOK!

Mischief at The Peacock Club

**A bold theft at the infamous Peacock Club.
Can Penelope solve it to save her own neck?**

1924 New York
Penelope "Pen" Banks has spent the past two years making ends meet by playing cards. It's another Saturday night at The Peacock Club, one of her favorite haunts, and she has

her sights set on a big fish, who just happens to be the special guest of the infamous Jack Sweeney.

After inducing Rupert Cartland, into a game of cards, Pen thinks it just might be her lucky night. Unfortunately, before the night ends, Rupert has been robbed—his diamond cuff links, ruby pinky ring, gold watch, and wallet...all gone!

With The Peacock Club's reputation on the line, Mr. Sweeney, aided by the heavy hand of his chief underling Tommy Callahan, is holding everyone captive until the culprit is found.

For the promise of a nice payoff, not to mention escaping the club in one piece, Penelope Banks is willing to put her unique mind to work to find out just who stole the goods.

This is a prequel novella to the *Penelope Banks Murder Mysteries* series, taking place at The Peacock Club before Penelope Banks became a private investigator.

Access your book at the link below:
https://dl.bookfunnel.com/4sv9fir4h3

ALSO BY COLETTE CLARK

PENELOPE BANKS MURDER MYSTERIES

A Murder in Long Island

The Missing White Lady

Pearls, Poison & Park Avenue

Murder in the Gardens

A Murder in Washington Square

The Great Gaston Murder

A Murder After Death

A Murder on 34th Street

Spotting A Case of Murder

The Girls and the Golden Egg

Murder on the Atlantic

LISETTE DARLING GOLDEN AGE MYSTERIES

A Sparkling Case of Murder

A Murder on Sunset Boulevard

A Murder Without Motive

ABOUT THE AUTHOR

Colette Clark lives in New York and has always enjoyed learning more about the history of her amazing city. She decided to combine that curiosity and love of learning with her addiction to reading and watching mysteries. Her first series, **Penelope Banks Murder Mysteries** is the result of those passions. When she's not writing she can be found doing Sudoku puzzles, drawing, eating tacos, visiting museums dedicated to unusual/weird/wacky things, and, of course, reading mysteries by other great authors.

Join my Newsletter to receive news about New Releases and Sales!
https://dashboard.mailerlite.com/forms/148684/
72678356487767318/share

Printed in Great Britain
by Amazon

27058999R00145